PUFFIN BOOKS

THE COMPLETELY CHAOTIC CHRISTMAS OF LOTTIE BROOKS

THE COMPLETELY CHAOTIC CHRISTMAS OF LOTTIE BROOKS

KATIE KIRBY

PUFFIN

PUFFIN BOOKS

UK | USA | Canada | Ireland | Australia
India | New Zealand | South Africa

Puffin Books is part of the Penguin Random House group of companies
whose addresses can be found at global.penguinrandomhouse.com.

www.penguin.co.uk   www.puffin.co.uk   www.ladybird.co.uk

First published 2023
001

Text design by Kim Musselle
Printed and bound in Great Britain by Clays Ltd, Elcograf S.p.A.

The authorized representative in the EEA is Penguin Random House Ireland,
Morrison Chambers, 32 Nassau Street, Dublin D02 YH68

A CIP catalogue record for this book is available from the British Library

HARDBACK
ISBN: 978–0–241–64717–2

TRADE PAPERBACK
ISBN: 978–0–241–67687–5

All correspondence to:
Puffin Books
Penguin Random House Children's
One Embassy Gardens, 8 Viaduct Gardens, London SW11 7BW

Happy Christmas to Cara and Sophia.

This one is for you x

WEDNESDAY 30 NOVEMBER

Let it be known that I, Charlotte Rose Brooks, love Christmas. And when I say 'I love it', I mean **I REALLY LOVE IT**, because let's face it – how could you not?!

Here are a few of my favourite festive things . . .

1. Presents.

2. Fairy lights.

3. Oven food.

4. Chocolate.

5. Ferrero Rochers (technically also a chocolate but I feel it needs its own category because it's the holy grail of chocolate wizardry).

I don't mean to sound arrogant, but she's not wrong!

6. Snuggling on the sofa and watching Christmas movies.

7. Parents getting tipsy and saying 'yes' to things they would normally say 'no' to.

The last one is one of the best. Everyone gets into the Christmas spirit and feels like they can't bear to disappoint.

For example, try out some of these . . .

'Mum, can I have (insert festive treat you want here) for (insert mealtime here)?'

'Dad, can I have (insert amount of money you want here) for (insert festive-related activity here)?'

'Mum, can I stay up until (insert new bedtime here) because I want to watch (insert festive film/tv programme here)?'

TOP TIP: The closer it gets to Christmas, the more effective the above questions are.

If you are not already convinced, why not?! Christmas is all sorts of awesome and that's just a fact and I have a feeling in my bones that this one is going to be particularly epic, don't you agree?

☐ A. Yes

☐ B. No

☐ C. Hmmm . . . I'm about 50:50, TBH

☐ D. Stop waffling, Lottie, and just TELL US
WHAT'S BEEN HAPPENING SINCE YOUR
LAST DIARY!!!

OK, JEEZ! I can't believe you picked D?! Keep your knickers on, I was just getting round to it. Incidentally, isn't it strange that we know each other so well that I can practically read your mind! Spoooooooky.

So, how about a little summary . . .

You may remember that I made friends with my EX-B (Ex-Boyfriend) Daniel again, just before I found out that my annoying little brother purposely tried to sabotage my relationship with my HFB (Handsome French Boy) Antoine. So now the love triangle is officially BACK ON – cripes.

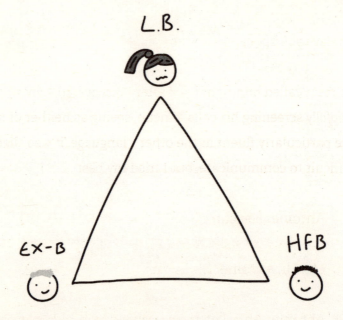

L.B.

EX-B   HFB

I've pre-anticipated all your questions, so for ease I'll answer them interview-style:

Q: What happened to Toby after you found out? Did you actually kill him?

A: As much as I really felt like killing him, my parents are strangely fond of him, so alas, Toby lives to see another day. I did spend about thirty minutes bashing him round the head with a pillow though. I'd like to say it taught him a lesson but that's probably untrue. It has taught *me* a lesson, though, and that is to **ALWAYS, ALWAYS BE DEEPLY SUSPICIOUS OF SMELLY LITTLE BROTHERS!**

Q: Have you spoken to Antoine since?

A: Yes! I called him right back after I discovered Toby was so *helpfully* screening his calls. I mean, seeing as neither of us are particularly fluent in the other's language, it was slightly difficult to communicate, but I tried my best . . .

Antoine: *Bonjour!*

Me: Hi, Antoine. It's Lottie!

Antoine: Ahh, Lottie, *ma petite* dustbin! I have been worrying for you in my bones.

Me: Erm . . . I'm not a little dustbin, but whatever. I just called to say I found out that Toby hasn't been passing on your messages. I'm so sorry. I hope you don't think I've been ignoring you!

Antoine: Ahh, Toby, he say you in hospital all covered in boils that are full of the disgustin' pus?

Me: Yes, that's right – I mean, NO! He was lying, I was just away on a school trip. I definitely don't have any horrible pus-filled boils.

Antoine: *Ohh là là, très bon* news! I so glad you have recover well from this boils?

Me: Look, I never had any boils but never mind, it's not important. How are you, Antoine?

Antoine: Now I 'ear you are out of 'ospital I am happy as a pineapple in a pile of poop!

I'll level with you here. I really didn't know what to say to this, so there was a rather awkward two-minute silence while I tried and failed to stop visualizing a pineapple in a pile of poop. (Why would it be happy?! What a strange analogy?!)

FYI I'm NOT happy. This is absolutely horrible!

I thought I'd better bring the conversation back to safer topics . . .

Me: *J'aime la* cheese.

Antoine: Ahhh, *j'aime la* cheese.
(ETC., ETC.)

Q: How about Daniel? You seemed to get on pretty well at your fireworks birthday party . . .

A: We did! All is good with Daniel now – phew! If I'm honest, I think there *may* be some feelings left between us, but as we've had a rocky relationship so far, we are both a bit reluctant for any more drama. So, I guess we are just trying to enjoy being friends for now, which is much simpler all round and means we get to hang out and stuff, which is **AWESOME**.

Tomorrow after school he's coming along with Theo and the rest of my gang to get some chips at Frydays – as *friends*, because it's nice to have *friends* and to hang out with your *friends*, isn't it?

I'll answer that for you – Yes. Yes, it is, Lottie.

THURSDAY 1 DECEMBER

7.32 a.m.

Woke up early to give the hammies their Advent calendars.
I make mini ones every year and in each tiny pocket I put a
pumpkin seed. It does mean that they get the exact same
thing every day, but they are too stupid to mind.

Then I ran downstairs as fast as I could because I wanted to get to my calendar before Toby and totally spoil it for him by revealing what is behind door number one. Some people might say that was a bit mean, but I say it's just a perk of being a big sister!

Sat down to eat breakfast and then Mum and Dad came in laughing and rubbing their hands together. They go, 'Notice anything . . . funny?'

I went back to eating my Cheerios. 'Nope.'

More laughter. 'Have you noticed anything . . . different, Toby?' said Mum.

Toby doesn't even reply as he's glued to the iPad watching other people play Minecraft on YouTube.

'Look up!' said Dad, clearly growing impatient.

I looked at the ceiling and there is one of those creepy Elf on the Shelf things hanging from a helium balloon with a note in its arms . . .

'He's called GAVIN?!' I said.

'Yes, what's wrong with that?' said Mum.

'It's just a strange name for an elf, that's all.'

'Well, what would you expect an elf to be called?'

'I dunno . . . maybe something like . . . Jolly Sparkle-Pants.'

Toby burst out laughing. 'Yeh, or Ding-Dong Frosty-Balls.'

'Well, ours is called Gavin, OK?' said Mum.

'That's boring,' protested Toby.

'Well, I suppose we could compromise and maybe give Gavin another na–' started Dad.

'GAVIN SPARKLE-BALLS!' shouted Toby.

Bella giggled and clapped her hands together.

I shrugged. 'Fine by me!'

Mum sighed. 'Welcome to the madhouse, Gavin Sparkle-Balls!'

4.35 p.m.

In tutor time, Mr Peters announced that our form would be doing a Secret Santa and tomorrow we would be picking names out of the hat to see who you would be buying a present for. There is a five-pound limit, and the gifts will be given out on the last day of term.

'I hope I get one of you guys,' Jess said to me, Poppy, Amber and Molly on our way to our first lesson.

'Yeh, me too. Knowing my luck, I'll probably get stuck with Burger Tom,' I said.

Molly smiled. 'That wouldn't be so bad – you could just buy him a Big Mac.'

'Ewww, it would be stone-cold and an absolute state after you'd carried it all the way to school.' Amber grimaced.

'He'd probably still eat it though!' said Jess.

I laughed. 'True!'

'Well, let's all cross our fingers we get each other, then we know we will get nice gifts,' said Jess.

I really hope she's right, although TBH Amber would probably be a nightmare to buy for, as what can you get her that she doesn't already have?! I guess in an ideal world I'd get Jess. I know her so well and she's really easy-going so she likes everything. ☺

FRIDAY 2 DECEMBER

Gavin Sparkle-Balls nearly killed me today!

I was making my way down to get breakfast in the
pitch-black because my school starts at the ridiculous hour
of 8.30, which is way too dark and cold in the middle of the
winter (but that's a rant for another time), and before I knew
what was going on I skidded across the kitchen floor.

'OWWWWW!' I screamed.

No one came to help me.

'OWWWWWWWWW!' I screamed again.

Nothing.

'I think I've broken my neck!'

Nothing.

'I'm pretty sure I'm dying!'

Nothing.

Finally, the Fun Police appeared in the kitchen and turned on the lights.

'Oh, for goodness' sake, Lottie, you've totally ruined today's scene,' said Mum.

As my eyes adjusted to the light, I saw that I was lying in white powdery stuff. On closer inspection, it appeared to be flour.

'Why is the floor covered in flour?'

'It's not flour, it's snow; Gavin was making snow angels in it.'

I said, 'I could have broken a bone! I think you'll find that covering the floor in flour –'

'I think you mean snow.'

'*Sorry*, I mean covering the floor in "snow" is a serious breach of health-and-safety regulations!'

Dad said, 'Don't you mean ELF-and-safety regulations?' and then he laughed for about ten minutes at his own joke.

TBH, I found it pretty funny too, but as I was meant to be in pain with my severely twisted ankle and broken neck, I just had to hobble over to the kitchen table and eat my Cheerios looking miserable (with my head tilted to the side), which was actually pretty difficult and meant I dribbled milk all down my PJs.

I tried to insist to Mum that I was in too much pain to go to school but she just handed me a couple of ibuprofen and practically shoved me out of the door. CHARMING! I think she's still a bit cross at me for ruining Gavin's snow angels for Toby and Bella. I mean Toby, fair enough, but Bella doesn't have a clue what's going on . . . Her favourite pastime is trying to eat her own hands!

4.24 p.m.

First thing Amber said to me when I arrived at school was, 'God, Lottie – not sure if you've noticed but you seem to have developed a serious dandruff problem . . . Maybe you need to start using a medicated shampoo?'

'What?! I don't have –' I began.

Oh. The Flour.

Due to my near-death experience, I had not had time to look in the mirror properly before I had been rudely pushed out of the front door. I took my ponytail out, ran my hands through my hair and gave it a good shake. Luckily this helped with the flour issue but not with the trying-to-look-like-a-normal-human problem because it turns out that the flour works a bit like a volumizing product (which incidentally might be good in preparation for a special event . . . but not exactly at 8.45 in the morning just before science).

Amber was now looking absolutely disgusted.

'Relax. It's only flour,' I told her. 'Blame my mum. No, actually, blame Gavin Sparkle-Balls!'

'Gavin Sparkle-Balls?!'

'Don't ask.'

'I wasn't going to,' huffed Amber dismissively. 'I don't have time for your ridiculous life today.'

CHARMING.

After school I went to the loos to check my hair was looking OK (and free of flour). I gave my fringe a brush and applied some cherry-tinted lip balm, a quick stroke of mascara to my lashes, then I ran to the gates to meet the girls.

'Oooh, Lottie – look at you!' said Molly.

'What?!' I said.

'You put make-up on!' said Amber.

Trust them to notice the *tiniest* of details.

'So?!'

'So, I thought you and Daniel were just *"friends"*?' said Poppy, making quote marks with her fingers.

'We are,' I said, trying to sound disinterested.

'Well, you are looking pretty fancy for meeting a *"friend"*!' Amber smirked.

Honestly, I can't win. This morning I looked disgusting and now I look too fancy?!

'Oh, leave her alone,' said Jess. 'You look pretty, Lottie. Ignore them.'

I smiled at her, and then, keen to change the subject, said, 'Right, come on, let's go or the queue will be massive.'

We walked to Frydays and saw Daniel and Theo standing outside, waiting for us.

'What took you so long?' shouted Theo as we approached.

'Blame Lottie!' said Amber. 'She was in the toilets doing –'

I had my back to Daniel, so I gave her my best Death Stare. I didn't want her to tell them I had being putting make-up on – it would look like I was doing it for him! Which I wasn't . . . obviously. I was doing it for myself . . . obviously.

'She, er . . . she was . . .' Amber stuttered, trying to think on her feet.

Thinking she was being helpful, Poppy jumped in and finished the sentence for her . . .

OMG!!!!!!!!!!!!!!!

Tumbleweed silence, followed by laughter

I could feel the heat rise to my face. I wanted to die.

What on earth was Poppy thinking???!

'WHAT?!' said Poppy, shrugging at everyone's reaction. 'Don't be immature, guys, everyone poos – it's nothing to be embarrassed about.'

Theo doubled over, with tears in his eyes. 'Tru dat. Was it a good one, Lottie?'

By now, my face was so red it was practically pulsating. Everyone was silent, waiting for me to describe my pooing experience, despite the fact that I wasn't even doing one.

'I . . . well . . . yes, it was rather –'

'Shall we get in the queue and order then?' interrupted Jess.

I had never been so glad to see everyone shuffle away. God knows what could've come out of my mouth if it wasn't for Jess. I followed them into Frydays and stood right at the back to give the blood a chance to drain away from my face. I hate blushing so much! It just draws even more attention to me. URGH. Someone needs to invent a cure for it.

Once we had ordered and collected our chips (and my face had returned to a normal shade), we went to the green outside. It was cold but bright, so we decided to sit on the wall to eat. I sat on the end next to Molly, and Daniel came and sat at the other side of me.

I felt I really needed to say something to him to get over the awkwardness of earlier.

'Good chips?' I asked.

'The best,' he said, smiling as he dipped one in curry sauce and put it in his mouth.

'What are you up to this weekend?'

'Nothing exciting really. We have family round for lunch on Saturday and a footie game on Sunday. You?'

'Not sure yet, hopefully a chilled one but I'm sure my

parents will try and drag me out somewhere awful.'

He laughed and then we both fell silent. I tried desperately to think of something else to say but my mind was completely blank.

'Don't worry about earlier, by the way,' said Daniel eventually.

'What do you mean?'

'I mean – Poppy was right – everybody does poo.' Then he turned to me with a cheeky grin. 'I don't think any less of you for it.'

I laughed and threw a chip at him. 'Thanks – that's big of you!'

He looked at me in mock outrage. 'Erm – two problems . . . Firstly, you just got a greasy stain on my blazer and secondly, that's a waste of excellent chips!'

'OOPS!' I laughed. He wasn't wrong. 'You know . . . I'm really glad we are mates again,' I said shyly.

'Me too, Lottie.'

Then we finished our chips, chatting about nothing and everything all at once.

THOUGHT OF THE DAY:
Do you really think that after everything that has happened between us, me and D could be proper friends again?? I really hope so!

SATURDAY 3 DECEMBER

AAAAAARRRRGHHHHH!! Guess what??!?!

I had a very bad dream last night . . .

I was about to take part in a doughnut-eating competition
– South-East regional finals – I was dead nervous and then
Daniel appeared at the front of the crowd, jumped up on
to the stage, walked up to me and said, 'Good luck, Lottie –
you can do this!' – and then he KISSED ME and the kiss was
AMAZING!

Amazing kiss + plate of doughnuts = winning at life

I know what you are thinking – that sounds pretty good actually, so why did she say it was a bad dream?

Well, for two reasons . . .

1. Me and Daniel are just friends and friends don't kiss each other on the mouth – do they?! So now I'm feeling mega confused.

2. After the kiss, I was too distracted to concentrate on the competition so I only managed to eat five doughnuts. I was annoyed because the winner got a Harry Styles duvet cover (one of those ones where his head was the pillow) and the chance to compete at the Internationals in Hawaii! I'm not quite sure which I was most gutted about, TBH.

7.52 a.m.

Decided to message Jess:

> **ME:** Do you think if you dream something then it means you want it to happen?

JESS: No. I once dreamt that I died by drowning in an empty swimming pool filled with baby bunny rabbits and I don't want to die! 💀

ME: But I guess if you had to die, drowning in a pool of baby bunny rabbits would be a good way to go . . . 🐰🐰🐰

JESS: True . . . but I also had a dream where I mysteriously grew another head, and the other head was really mean and called me names like 'Idiot Face', and I definitely don't want to grow another mean head – do I?!

ME: Errr . . . do you always have such traumatic dreams, Jess?

JESS: Not always. Last night I dreamt I was a teaspoon. That was all right but pretty boring. Not much drama going on in the cutlery drawer, TBH. 🍴

ME: Has anyone ever told you you're a weirdo??

JESS: Takes one to know one! Why are you asking about my dreams anyway?

ME: Oh, I just had a dream that I kissed Daniel last night and I was worried it meant that maybe I still like him. Glad to know it doesn't!

JESS: Hang on a minute . . . That's different.

ME: How?!

JESS: Well, you used to like Daniel as more than a friend . . . you've kissed him before . . . and you liked it. And now you've dreamt about kissing him again, which can only mean one thing . . . You LURRRRRRRVE him, you want to KISSSSS him, and you want to MAAAAARRY him.

ME: You are being very immature, Jess, so I'm going to have to go now. BYE!

JESS: 💋 😝

10.24 a.m.

Went downstairs and found that Gavin S-B had been frozen inside a big block of ice. Personally, I think he is just attention-seeking, plus my ankle still hurts, so I am choosing to ignore his silly exploits. Toby, on the other hand, is in the garden trying to smash him free using one of Dad's golf clubs.

I assume the Fun Police wouldn't be too happy about it, but they are busy having their yearly argument about whether it's too early to get a Christmas tree so they haven't noticed.

It goes something like this . . .

1. Mum thinks it's too early to get a real tree as it will be dead by Christmas Day.

2. Dad thinks it will be fine and that Mum is a Scrooge.

3. Mum says, 'If you want to put up a tree in the first week of December you should get a fake one.'

28

4. Dad looks up fake trees and suggests one that costs £29.99 on classychristmastrees.com.

5. Mum says that if you want to get a real-looking fake tree you need to spend about 500 quid.

6. Dad says, 'YOU ARE HAVING AN ABSOLUTE LAUGH!'

7. Mum says it will pay for itself in a few years' time!

8. Dad says he doesn't really like fake trees anyway . . .

9. Mum says neither does she . . .

10. Dad puts 'It's Beginning to Look a Lot Like Christmas' on the Sonos and starts singing along really badly.

11. Mum says, 'Fine, let's go and get the blimmin' tree then!' just to shut him up.

12. We all go out in the freezing cold and spend far too long debating which tree to get.

13. Dad complains about how expensive it is.

14. The tree turns out to be far too big for its allocated position.

15. Everyone blames each other.

16. Dad saws off the top while swearing.

17. We put the tree up and decorate it.

18. It looks terrible.

(19.) Everyone agrees it's the best tree we've ever had (even though it's not).

(20.) Mum secretly redecorates the tree when we are all in bed.

(21.) The tree is completely dead by Christmas Eve.

(22.) Mum says, 'I told you so!'

(23.) Dad swears again.

(24.) The End.

(3.34 p.m.)

The tree has been purchased in accordance with steps 12–15.

Dad is currently sawing the top off as per step 16.

I'm busy scoffing Ferrero Rochers. Might need to add this in as a new step, TBF . . .

Dad has got the box of decorations out of the loft and is currently trying to untangle the lights while swearing (yes, again – I'm going to have to have a word with him about his bad language), Mum is guzzling mulled wine, Toby is playing golf with the baubles, Bella is trying to eat the fairy, and I'm looking at my phone and trying to pretend this is not my family.

(This drawing would prob make quite an authentic Christmas card, don't ya think?!)

4.55 p.m.

Tree is decorated and as per step 18 all the decorations have been put on one side and it looks awful.

'I think this is the best tree we've ever had!' says Dad.

I laugh.

'What?!' he says to me.

'You say that EVERY year.'

'No, I don't!'

'You do, actually, Dad, and Mum always secretly redecorates it when we are in bed.'

'I most certainly do not!' says Mum.

Dad raises his eyebrows. 'Well, Laura, you can't really deny that ...'

'Well, Bill, you can't deny that the tree will be dead by

Christmas Eve like ALWAYS.'

And so it goes on – they are SO predictable.

We have all just realized that Bella quite likes the Christmas tree and when I say 'quite likes' I mean 'wants to destroy'.

SUNDAY 4 DECEMBER

7.34 a.m.

What a surprise. Woke up, went downstairs and the tree looks completely different!

Quizzed Mum on it and she said it must have been the elf – good old Gavin Sparkle-Balls, eh? An elf of many talents!

12.35 p.m.

Everything was suspiciously quiet and calm in the house, so I went to investigate and found Mum in the kitchen drinking coffee and flicking through the papers.

'What are you doing?' I asked, obviously sounding surprised.

'Bella's napping, Toby's at a friend's and I'm just enjoying five minutes of peace – is that OK?'

'Yes, but – I mean, it's December. Shouldn't you be more stressed out?'

She laughed. 'I've not told you the news yet, have I? This Christmas, Granny and Grandad have decided to stay up north with your aunties – so for the first time ever it will be just the five of us. Won't that be nice?'

'Erm. Sounds a bit boring, TBH.'

'Yes, well, you aren't the one doing all the cooking and waiting on everyone hand and foot, are you?'

'I suppose not . . . They will still get us presents, won't they?'

'I should expect so.'

'PHEW!'

I'm not sure how I feel about having a small family Christmas. I mean, how will it be any different to any other time of the year? It feels a bit sad if I'm honest and I think I'll really miss not having Granny and Grandad around. At least Grandad won't steal the remote and force us to watch *Coronation Street* though.

Was sitting in the armchair doing some highly confidential research when I suddenly felt the hot, foul breath of my horrible little brother on my neck . . .

OMG!!! I actually can't put up with this any longer.

I told the Fun Police that one of us has to go – me or him . . . and guess what they said: 'Both of you!'

How blimmin' rude is that?

MONDAY 5 DECEMBER

7.25 a.m.

Gavin had a toileting malfunction this morning. He had pooped chocolate chips all over the kitchen worktops.

I gathered them up and chucked them on top of my cereal.

'URGH, you just put poo on your cereal?!?!' said Toby, looking absolutely disgusted.

'It's not actually poo, you wally!'

'Are you sure?'

'Of course I'm sure.' I took a big spoonful of cornflakes and chocolate chips and ate it.

Poor kid probably thinks the elf is real?! As if I'd voluntarily eat elf poo!!

$$\boxed{\text{4.33 p.m.}}$$

Saw Daniel on the way to school and I felt all shy and embarrassed, so I put my head down and pretended not to see him. Damn my stupid dream for confusing me like this!!

In morning tutor time, Mr Peters started waving a Santa hat around.

'Good morning, Eight Green! Write your names on the slip of paper in front of you and then fold it up and pop it in here, please. It's time to draw names for the hotly anticipated Secret Santa!'

I wrote my name on the slip of paper, folded it up small, gave it a kiss and went up to Mr Peters's desk to put it in the hat.

'Good luck, Miss Brooks,' he said.

'Thanks, sir.'

'I hope I get someone good,' I whispered to Poppy as I sat back down.

'I don't really care who I get. I just want someone good to get me,' she replied.

'Good point.'

'Right, everybody,' said Mr Peters, 'looks like we have a full house, so I'll come round with the hat and everyone can pick a name out. And remember, it's called SECRET Santa, i.e. you are not meant to tell ANYBODY which name you get. OK?'

'OK, sir,' we all chimed.

I crossed my fingers underneath the desk and watched as my classmates started drawing out names. Some of them unfolded the paper immediately, grinning or grimacing in response to the name they got. Others snaffled the paper into their pockets or pencil cases to check it later in private.

'YES!' exclaimed Amber, punching the air.

Molly smiled when she read her name and Poppy did a very good poker face so I couldn't tell if she was pleased or disappointed.

'I'm going to check mine at home later,' Jess said.

'Me too,' I agreed. 'Let's FaceTime and do it together?'

'Deal.'

When it was my turn I rifled around and picked a piece of paper right from the bottom of the hat, held it tight in my fist and then put it into the front pocket of my rucksack. It was sooooo tempting to have a quick peek, but I managed to stop myself.

When I got home, I ran upstairs to my room and called Jess.

'Have you done it yet?' she asked when she answered.

'No. You?'

'No. So, shall we do it together?'

'Yes. Hang on a sec,' I said as I propped my phone up against some books on my desk and rummaged around on my bed for the folded bit of paper.

'OK, I'm ready,' said Jess.

'Me too.'

'Let's do it on three.'

'One . . . two . . . three . . .' we both counted together and opened up the paper at the same time.

'WOOHOO!!' I said, punching the air.

This is what the paper said . . .

I looked back at my phone with a massive grin on my face . . .

Jess was grinning too. 'So?' she said.

'Well, I can't tell you who I got, can I?'

'Ha. Is it anyone good?'

'They're . . . OK, I guess. How about you?'

'If you're not telling me then I'm not telling you,' she said and laughed.

'Fair enough, I guess . . . Now to get planning . . .'

'Deffo! See you tomoz, Lotts!'

'Yep – see ya!'

THOUGHT OF THE DAY:
I'm thrilled to get Jess. It couldn't have gone ANY better, could it?! I mean, what are the chances that out of thirty-two of us in the class I got my bestest BFF?!

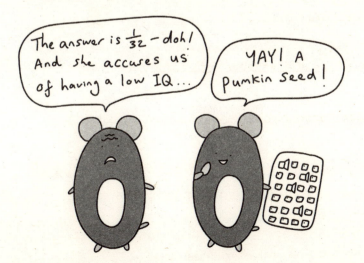

TUESDAY 6 DECEMBER

Canteen at lunchtime . . .

Walked in, sat down with The Queens of Eight Green, who were
already assembled and halfway through their cheese paninis
(side note: some days I think maybe we should change our gang
name to Cheese Paninis 4 Life or something like that) – anyway,
back to the point – and Jess nudged me. 'Look who's behind
you and look what he's doing . . .' she said, pointing behind her.

I turned my head and looked as slyly as I could over my
shoulder.

'Oh my God!' I said.

'What?! What is it, Lottie?' asked Molly, looking confused.

'It's Daniel and he's eating a doughnut,' explained Jess.

'So?! What's wrong with that?! Since when was eating a
doughnut illegal?!' asked Amber, looking bored.

'Shhhhhh,' I whispered, 'there's nothing wrong with eating a doughnut, it's just that at the weekend I had a weird dream that I was at a doughnut-eating competition and Daniel was there cheering me on and then he . . . he . . . he kissed me!'

'OOOOH, THAT'S EXCITING!' said Molly, clapping her hands together.

Amber rolled her eyes. 'You have a very warped view of what's exciting, Molly.'

And then with horror I heard Daniel's voice directly behind me: 'What are you girls talking about? What's exciting?'

Amber grinned, suddenly coming to life. 'Oh yummy, is that a nice doughnut, Daniel?'

'Um, yeh, it's pretty good,' he replied, looking suspicious.

'Lottie REALLY enjoys doughnuts.'

I gave her a Death Stare.

'Lottie has good taste,' said Daniel, smiling.

45

'She even dreams about them sometimes,' continued Amber. 'Maybe you should give her a bite . . .'

'Errr, OK . . . would you like a bite, Lottie?'

I didn't know what to do. It did look really good, but I absolutely did not want to take a bite in front of the girls – and especially Amber, who was enjoying this encounter *far* too much.

'No, thank you, I'm actually quite full,' I said.

Amber raised her eyebrows. 'Surely you can manage one *tiny* bite?'

'It is a good one,' said Daniel, offering the half-eaten doughnut to me.

'Oh, fine!' I grabbed it and tried to take a little bite, but I must have bitten into the jammy area as it all squirted and ran down my chin, dripping on to my shirt and tie.

'We can't take you anywhere, can we, Lottie? What a mess!
Has anyone got any baby wipes?' said Amber, pretending to
scold me like a toddler.

The other girls were all trying to hold in their giggles and
Daniel just looked a bit disappointed that I'd clearly
massacred his lovely doughnut.

'Well, glad you enjoyed it,' he said, taking the squished
remains back as I tried to wipe the sticky jam off my face.

'Um, yeh, it was . . . Sorry about the . . .' I stuttered.

He smiled. 'It's fine, honest, I've gotta go – see ya soon.'

We all said goodbye and I watched as he walked through the canteen and disappeared through the doors.

'I think that went REALLY well,' said Poppy, and the rest of the girls erupted into fits of laughter.

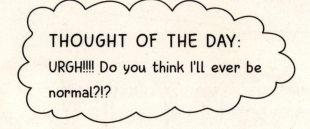

THOUGHT OF THE DAY:
URGH!!!! Do you think I'll ever be normal?!?

WEDNESDAY 7 DECEMBER

Toby came home absolutely thrilled. They held auditions today for the Nativity, which is to be performed at our local church on the Sunday before Christmas, and he got the part of Sheep Two. Apparently the audition involved 'baaing' in a realistic way and Toby excelled at it.

Mum said, 'Well, we clearly have a very talented family: Lottie the singing crab/award-winning triangle player and Toby the realistic-sounding sheep – I wonder what Bella will surprise us with when she is older?!'

We all turned to look at Bella, who at that moment decided to shout 'bum'!

'Oh my gosh!' said Mum. 'She's only eleven months old and she just said *Mum* – that's amazing!'

Did she not hear what I heard?! 'I hate to break it to you, Mother . . . but she actually said *bum*.'

49

'Yeh – she definitely said *bum*,' said Toby, laughing.

'No . . . it was *Mum*, wasn't it, Bella? Can you say it again . . . can you say *Mum*?'

'BUM!' said Bella, more clearly this time, while bashing her rattle excitedly on Mum's head.

'Ow, Bella, that hurt . . . You mean *Mum*, don't you, sweetie? Mum! Mummy! Mama!'

We all looked at Bella, waiting for her response . . .

Me and Toby completely lost it at this point and collapsed on the floor holding our tummies. Mum continued to try and correct her (unsuccessfully), while also trying to protect herself from a rattle-based head injury (also unsuccessfully). Sometimes I do worry that Bella is possessed by some sort of demon?!

7.12 p.m.

WhatsApp convo with Antoine:

ANTOINE: Hello, dustbin! How is you?

ME: Hi, Antoine. I'm good, thank you. How are you?

ANTOINE: I be feeling a very large excitement for the visit of Beard Man!

ME: Ahh me too. I love Christmas! What are you asking . . . Beard Man for this year?

ANTOINE: A spiritual experience involving an orang-utan and a PlayStation 5.

ME: Wow. Well, I will keep my fingers crossed for ya.

ANTOINE: What does Lottie do for Christ Mouse this year?

ME: I am having a nice quiet Christmas at home. It's a shame we live so far apart as we could have invited you and your family around for a glass of eggnog!

ANTOINE: A glass of egg?

ME: Well, it's a drink . . .

ANTOINE: You drink eggs from a glass?

ME: Not just eggs, it's got alcohol in it too . . .

ANTOINE: You drink alcoholic eggs from a glass?

ME: Yes . . . well, not me personally, I'm only thirteen, but my parents do.

ANTOINE: You English ones are a strange occurrence.

ME: I agree.

ANTOINE: OK, *bonne nuit.* I go off to ask *ma famille* if they like to come to England for Christ Mouse and drink alcoholic eggs from a glass with la *Brooks famille.* x

ME: Ha ha. *Bonne nuit,* Antoine x

THOUGHT OF THE DAY:

That was a bit weird. Did I just accidentally invite Antoine here for Christmas?! Hopefully it's just a translation issue as I'm not sure the Fun Police would be too happy about his entire family turning up in Brighton to drink alcoholic eggs. LOL.

THURSDAY 8 DECEMBER

Woke up this morning and went downstairs to find Toby
with his hands covering his mouth in shock. Gavin
Sparkle-Balls was standing on the kitchen table leaning
up against a glass filled with bright yellow liquid.

'Lottie! He's weed into a glass!!'

I sighed. 'Honestly, Toby. You are so dumb. It's obviously
not actual *wee*!! Mum's just put apple juice into a glass and
made it look like Gavin did it.'

'He did! He must have done. It looks exactly like proper wee!'

'Oh for goodness' sake,' I said, picking up the glass. 'It's apple
juice – I'll show you.'

I took a big gulp and Toby looked at me, his eyes wide.

Slowly I realized something was wrong . . .

It was warm.

It was NOT apple juice.

I spat it out across the table.

Toby looked ridiculously pleased with himself. I had never felt so disgusted in my entire life!

'I'M GOING TO KILL YOU!!!' I screamed, chasing him around the kitchen armed with a pear. (I do understand that pears aren't particularly threatening, but it was the first thing I could grab, OK?)

'You'll have to catch me first!' said Toby, laughing.

'You little . . . !' I raised my arm and threw the pear as hard
as I could, hitting him on the shoulder.

'Didn't hurt!'

'What's going on?' Mum and Dad had come rushing in to see
what all the commotion was about.

'She's throwing pears at me!' said Toby like this was all my
fault.

'It was a pear – singular! And he deserved it.'

'I don't think there is any excuse for throwing fruit at people at 7.23 a.m., regardless of the quantity,' said Mum.

'But Toby . . . Toby –' I could barely speak; I put my fingers in my mouth, trying to claw out any remaining traces of my brother's urine – 'he . . . he made me drink his wee!'

Mum looked horrified. 'What on earth? Toby – is this true?!'

Toby smirked. 'RELAX. It's just water and food colouring. I'm not that *gross*.'

'But it was warm!' I argued.

He grinned. 'I microwaved it!'

I looked at Mum, open-mouthed. She was clearly finding the whole thing highly amusing. 'Toby,' she said, trying to look stern, 'that wasn't very kind, was it?'

'It was a good trick though, hey?' he replied.

'Really good!' said Dad, giving him a high-five.

I couldn't believe no one had any sympathy for what I'd just been through. 'Are you going to let him get away with this?!' I said, putting my hands on my hips.

Dear reader, they were all laughing too much to even give me an answer!!

THOUGHT OF THE DAY:
ARGHGGGGHGHH!!!
Why should I have to live like this?!
I am moving out of this madhouse
the second I turn eighteen!

FRIDAY 9 DECEMBER

Mother has been nagging me to write my Christmas list. I've told her it's in production but due to unforeseen circumstances has not been completed yet.

'What are the unforeseen circumstances?' she asked.

'Couldn't find a biro.'

'Well, what about that one right in front of you?'

'Oh right . . . yeh.'

Guess I'd better do it then.

Did my list . . .

Lottie's Christmas List:
1. Dyson Airwrap
2. Money

Handed it to Mum . . .

'What is this?!' she said.

'My Christmas list, like you asked for.'

She had a really sad look on her face. 'But you haven't even addressed it to Father Christmas . . .'

I rolled my eyes. 'Oh, come on, Mum, does it really matter?'

'Yes. It's plain bad manners. If you don't put some effort into it, then Father Christmas isn't likely to put much effort into your gifts either . . .'

'OK, OK, I'll do it again.'

Dear Father Christmas,

Hope all is well in the North Pole with you and Mrs Christmas? I feel for you at this time of year, with billions of letters to read and presents to deliver. How you do it all by yourself is really quite astounding . . . In fact, I can't think about it too much as it makes my brain want to explode! I hope you get a lovely break in January to recuperate – I hear the Bahamas is gorgeous at that time of year . . .

Anyway, I'm writing to tell you that I've been unbelievably well-behaved this year. In fact, some people would go as far as to say I've been positively charming! Don't believe the hype?? Why not read the following references from completely unbiased parties:

Mr Peters (form tutor) – Lottie is a popular and kind pupil. She is an absolute delight to teach. ~~However she would benefit from talking less, concentrating in class and remembering to do her homework on time.~~

Jess Williams (my BFF) – Decorum? Grace? Maturity? Humility? Lottie has got it all in spades – she's a shining example to teenagers everywhere!

Professor Squeakington (my hamster) – Provides great snacks and regularly refills the water bottle.

Could clean the cage a bit more often but hey, no one's perfect, are they? Any hamster would be proud to call her their owner.

Right, enough of the pleasantries. Let's get down to business . . .

I would be humbled and forever grateful if I could receive the following presents this Christmas:

1. A Dyson Airwrap.
2. Money. Lots of it.
3. Some sort of magic spell that makes my little brother less annoying, smelly and loud (totally get this may not be possible, but if you don't ask . . .)

Thanking you kindly in advance,

Charlotte Rose Brooks

PS We always leave you a G&T out along with the carrots and mince pie but last year I caught my father drinking it, which leads me to suspect he may have done so in previous years too – sorry about that!

Gave the new letter to Mum and she raised her eyebrows
so much I was a bit worried they would disappear into her
hairline, never to be seen again. Then she took it through to
the kitchen to show Dad.

'HOOOOOOOWWWW MUCH?!?!??!!' he roared.

I think half the street heard him.

I went downstairs to investigate and turns out he was
referring to the Dyson Airwrap.

'I'm not being funny, Lottie, but you have a perfectly good
hairdryer already.'

'This is not a hairdryer, Dad. It's a multi-styler. Do you want
to see a YouTube video of how it works?' I asked.

'Not really.'

I ignored him and loaded up a video for them to see on my
phone.

'Oh, it does look rather good,' said Mum, watching over my shoulder. 'See how lovely the curls come out.'

'Told you! It basically creates a spinning vortex of air so that –' I started to explain before I was rudely interrupted.

'A spinning vortex of air?! You are having a laugh. I'd expect it to make me a fry-up for breakfast for that money!'

Mum looked at me apologetically. 'I hate to say it but your dad's right, love. Unfortunately, it is a lot of money and it's not like you wear your hair down much, is it?'

I sighed. 'No, I suppose not.'

Mum smiled. 'Good girl, and maybe add a few slightly cheaper options to your Christmas list too, eh?'

'OK.'

Bit gutted but guess she had a point. I'm still keeping my fingers crossed that FC is feeling extra generous this year though.

Don't tell anyone this, as it makes me sound kind of immature, but I helped the hammies write their Christmas lists too! Tee hee.

SATURDAY 10 DECEMBER

(11.55 a.m.)

I'm lying on the sofa in my pyjamas, watching an incredibly enlightening YouTube video called 'Cats Stuck in Weird Places', when Mum comes in and says, 'Come on, Lottie, you need to get ready. We are leaving in twenty minutes.'

'What?! Where are we going?'

'We are going to see Father Christmas at the garden centre.'

'Mum, I'm thirteen years old! I don't want to go to the garden centre and sit on Santa's knee any more. It's embarrassing and TBH quite inappropriate.'

'Don't be silly, Lottie, you don't have to sit on his knee, but it's Bella's first Christmas, remember, and I want to get a nice Christmassy photo of you all together in the grotto. Plus, we need to post your letters in the North Pole Mailbox.'

I groaned. 'Well, thanks for telling me. I had plans today.'

'What plans? You are just lying on the sofa in your PJs.'

'Those were my plans! Now I'm going to have to get dressed and that disrupts my entire schedule.'

'Your entire schedule of what exactly?'

'Well at 12 p.m. I was going to eat some Super Noodles.'

'You can still do that if you are quick.'

'They don't taste as good when you are wearing proper clothes.'

'Oh, for goodness' sake, Lottie,' she said switching the TV off, 'go and get ready – and don't forget to brush your teeth.'

I stomped upstairs as loudly as I could – now I'll never get to find out if the ickle tabby kitten managed to get his head out of the Ben & Jerry's carton!

3.58 p.m.

Well, I'll tell you one thing for sure: Bella and Toby won't be getting much in their stockings this year.

The garden centre ended up being SUPER busy and we had to queue up for like 80 million years. Obviously, we were all complaining to Mum about it, which for some reason made her really grouchy.

When it was finally our turn they refused to let me into the grotto without paying, even though I said I didn't want a present, so Mum had to fork out for all three of us just to get the silly photo. We quickly realized it was NOT worth the money!

Father Christmas is supposed to be all Christmassy, right? Wrong. He was such a grump. Probably also annoyed with all the rude, irritating children he's had to see today.

He almost threw our presents at us. Toby got a megaphone, which he was pleased about. I got a sparkly tiara and Bella got an eyeshadow set. Mum was 'appalled' – she said that they were outdated and sexist and that anyone who thinks giving an eight-year-old a megaphone is a good idea should be arrested. I had to agree, but the eyeshadow was actually quite nice, so I swiped it off Bella before Mum threw it in the bin.

I assumed that Mum would want to leave after that, but she was still hell-bent on getting this photo of the three of us despite FC being more like the Grinch.

Bella, the good judge of character that she usually is, flatly refused to sit on his knee and whenever Mum tried to hand her to the Big Guy, she screamed the place down and started flailing her fists around.

Mum did not want to give up. 'Bella Brooks, will you calm down and let me take one quick photo – please?!'

I have no idea why she was speaking to her like she could understand complete sentences.

She finally managed to hand her over and you won't believe this part: Bella grabbed his beard and bit him really hard on the nose – next thing we know, FC is screaming too and blood is spurting out of his nostrils. The other kids behind us started crying and their parents were trying to shield their eyes from the gory scene. Meanwhile Toby had powered up his megaphone and decided to give the place a running commentary:

'SORRY FOR THE DELAY, EVERYBODY. MY SISTER HAS JUST BITTEN SANTA'S NOSE OFF. WE THANK YOU FOR YOUR PATIENCE AND WE WILL HOPEFULLY BE BACK UP AND RUNNING SHORTLY AFTER SANTA HAS RECEIVED MEDICAL ATTENTION.'

Could this get any worse?

Mum tried to apologize but FC wasn't really in the mood. Judging by all the blood, I'd say Bella's incisors must be as sharp as razor blades.

'Maybe you should tell Father Christmas to go and get a tetanus shot,' I whispered to Mum as she was gathering up our things in a panic.

'Oh, don't be silly, Lottie. It's not like Bella is a street cat.'

'Err, are you sure? They are pretty similar if you ask me. Anyway, what I'm asking is, can you say with a hundred per cent certainty that she doesn't have rabies?'

'Yes, Lottie! Your little sister **does not** have rabies, and I would be very grateful if you could stop saying such things out loud. If anyone hears you then they –'

'JUST A QUICK UPDATE FOR YOU, LADIES AND GENTLEMEN. UNFORTUNATELY, THERE IS A HIGH POSSIBILITY THAT SANTA HAS CONTRACTED RABIES. WE STRONGLY RECOMMEND THAT YOU DO NOT ALLOW YOUR CHILDREN TO APPROACH HIM UNLESS THEY HAVE BEEN VACCINATED!'

As me, Mum and Santa gawped at Toby, we watched the entire queue pack up their stuff and make a quick exit.

'Oh God, oh dear God,' Mum started muttering.

'Mum, just to let you know that a security guard, a paramedic and a rather cross-looking manager are making their way across the store right now,' I told her.

'Right. There is only one thing for it – **RUN!'**

And so we all pegged it out of the garden centre as fast as we could, got in the car and drove home, while Bella finally took her nap.

6.45 p.m.

Dad's back. He had a nice day apparently.

He asked, 'How was the Father Christmas visit?'

Me and Mum just sort of looked at each other, not really knowing quite what to say. Luckily Toby was on hand to summarize things pretty quickly with help from his megaphone.

BELLA GAVE HIM RABIES!!

THOUGHT OF THE DAY:

If Bella biting Father Christmas doesn't land her right at the top of the Naughty List, then I don't know what does! I mean, biting any random person is bad enough, but biting the guy in charge of festive gift distribution??? That's just madness.

We did get a pretty amazing shot though (deffo a framer) . . .

SUNDAY 11 DECEMBER

9.24 a.m.

Today I'm going shopping with the girls for our Secret Santa presents.

It's not like we can all shop together, as then we'd see what each other was getting, so we all agreed to meet up, then split up, then meet up again (at the churros stand so we could get churros as a reward for our hard work – yum!).

Obviously five pounds isn't a huge amount to spend so it's not like we can go browsing the fancy boutiques in The Lanes. On my hit list of places to go are Primark, Miniso, Tiger, H&M, Superdrug, WHSmith and the Lego Store. Jess likes stationery, smellies and cute stuff so hopefully I'll find some good options. I wanted to get her a few things too, rather than just one main thing (and I'm sure no one would really mind if I spent *slightly* more than a fiver – she is my bestie after all).

I'm home! There were so many cute cuddlies in Miniso, including a cat shaped like a doughnut, BUT it was way out of budget so I had to resist. I am really pleased with what I bought though. This is what I got her:

* A mini figure from the Lego Store that I made myself and looks just like Jess AND the accessory I got is a SLOTH! It's amazing – she will LOVE IT!

* Bubblegum-flavour Millions.

* Pink guava peel-off face mask.

* Watermelon-scented rubber.

It all added up to £6.69, which I hope is fine. If anyone questions it I'll say I got a discount code or there was an offer on.

Me and Jess shared some churros with chocolate dipping sauce after – they were SO good. She said she was really happy with her gift too so it was a great success!

MONDAY 12 DECEMBER

Today was **BRILLIANT!**

Probably the best day I've had in a long time. It was even better than the day that I discovered Bubble Tea and that's quite an accolade because we all know how much I LOVE the BT.

'Why was it so good, Lottie?' I can hear you all asking.

Well, firstly, school have started doing cheese AND bacon paninis and they are just the yummiest. I liked mine so much that I went and bought another one. I was very pleased to now have two lunch items on the menu to choose from – my mum will be less pleased when she checks my dinner-money account (especially when she sees the number of tray bakes I bought last week – oops!) but that's a worry for another day.

Secondly, Daniel came over to our table and plonked a doughnut down in front of me. 'Thought you might like this, Lottie!' he said, grinning and walking off again.

'Thank you,' I managed to shout after him.

The other TQOEG girls were left open-mouthed.

'OMG, Lottie,' said Jess, 'he deffo still has a crush on you.'

'Really? But we are meant to be friends now and I don't
want to over-complicate –'

'Look,' said Amber, 'do you still like the guy or what?'

'Yes . . . no . . . maybe . . . I'm so confused.'

'Lottie, you need to stop overthinking it,' said Molly. 'The way
I see it is that he clearly still likes you and you clearly still
have some feelings left too, so why not give it one more try
and see where it goes? It is nearly Christmas after all, and
Christmas is a time when you should say how you really
feel.'

I smiled. When did Molly get so wise?!

'You really think?

'Oh God,' said Amber, 'yes, we *really* think. In fact, I'll be positively *elated* if the two of you get back together. Now can we change the subject, please, as I'm about to fall asleep. Which of these new lip-gloss shades suits me best?'

While everyone was busy discussing the pros and cons of Strawberry Shimmer vs Electric Pink on Amber's complexion, I sat there quietly thinking. A warm feeling was stirring in my chest, because maybe – just maybe – it wasn't too late for me and Daniel after all.

Me and Daniel skipping off into the sunset (with doughnuts)

TUESDAY 13 DECEMBER

4.55 p.m.

Mum looked pretty stressed when I got home from school today. I asked her what was wrong, and she said, 'Everything, Lottie, everything!'

Then she explained that Granny and Grandad were thinking of coming here for Christmas after all because Auntie Emily and Auntie Claire are vegetarians, and they are refusing to cook a turkey. I thought that sounded like a good thing but apparently it's not because it's loads of extra work, and it won't be at all relaxing and Granny always complains about everything, and Grandad just sits on the sofa 24/7 and blah blah blah.

In other news, Toby is being very irritating. He seems to be taking his sheep role way too seriously and baaing constantly. He's even been watching videos of baaing sheep on YouTube.

Checked my emails and there was a rather strange message from Antoine . . .

> *Chère* Lottie,
>
> The most fantastic of news will be delivered to you via this electronic mail. Drum rolls please!!!
>
> *Ma famille* has gracious accepted the invitation

from your *famille* to come and drink alcoholic eggs in glasses!

Please inform your mother we are sincerely grateful that she will be catering for us all – it is so hospital of you, you kind-hearted badgers.

Please see below for our dietary commands:

Antoine: Pot Noodles and cheese. (LOL!)

Hugo: Every item of food must be yellow, except if it is a product of a pig or jam.

Ma mère: Fish in a dish. Several bottles of wine.

Mon père: VERY expensive steak. Banana milkshake. Cigarettes. NO sprout horror.

Is also possible for you to offer accommodations for us? Shall we bring sleeping utensils?

You is the most generous of dustbins,

Love of Antoine x

OH MY LIFE! What the heck has happened here? Does Antoine seriously think I have invited him to England for Christmas? And he wants to stay in our house?!

Decided to email Antoine back to double-check he won't turn up on our doorstep, as I'm not sure it would go down very well with *la famille* . . .

> Dear Antoine,
>
> Thanks for your hilarious email! I laughed a lot, you tricky trickster. I almost believed that you were seriously thinking of coming over to visit us. How ridiculous that would be!!
>
> HA HA. You are SO funny.
>
> You were obviously joking . . . weren't you?
>
> Lottie x

> Lottie, I does not understand why you could think

this was a joke? We are very looking forward to
having a traditional Englishman Christ Mouse
with you 😊

PS Will there be Rost-bif cooked to rubber?!
Ha ha!

WHAT IS HAPPENING?!?!

I don't mean to be rude, Antoine, but I think we
have our wires crossed. I was talking about
eggnog in a generic way. I was not asking you to
come round and try some.

Just to be 100 per cent clear . . .

YOU ARE NOT INVITED HERE FOR CHRISTMAS!

No offence. Our house is much too small for
you all to stay and if I'm being entirely honest,
we barely even know you and don't have a lot in
common (except cheese).

PS I tried a sip of eggnog once and it's very disgusting; it is NOT a reason to visit England.

Phew. Feel relieved now. That may have been a tad rude, but it was the only way.

HA! Now it is your turn to be a funny one. Imagine you invites someone to a Christmas experience involving eggs and then a change of the mind! That would be very rude and mean. Are you a rude and mean one? I think not!

I do understand about your mini house size, but don't worry, we don't need much space. We are all small dimensions of the body. I could even sleep in a wardrobe or sitting up in a chair?

Our flight details are below . . .

Sunday 25 December
Depart Paris Charles de Gaulle: 9.30 a.m.
Arrive London Gatwick: 11.35 a.m.

Tuesday 27 December

Depart London Gatwick: 16.45 p.m.

Arrive Paris Charles de Gaulle: 18.40 p.m.

I have excitement of the bum to see you soonest!!

NO! NO! NOOOOOOOOOOOOOOOO!!!!!!!

The Fun Police are going to kill me!!!!!!!!!!!!

(7.33 p.m.)

TQOEG WhatsApp group:

ME: Something SERIOUS has happened!!!

JESS: ?!?!??!

ME: So . . . basically I'm actually seriously worried that Antoine might SERIOUSLY be ACTUALLY coming to visit me at Christmas – as in, coming here – IN ACTUAL PERSON!!!

POPPY: Are you actually seriously worried OR are you seriously actually worried??

MOLLY: Because there is a big difference, you know . . .

ME: Guys, I'm actually being serious!!!

AMBER: Well, if you were actually being serious then why didn't you just say?

JESS: Yeh, I mean, from what you said, I assumed that you were being unactually unserious.

MOLLY: And when you say that he's coming here in 'actual person' are you sure you've got your facts straight . . . or could he actually be coming here as, for example, a cardboard cut-out?

POPPY: Ooh, that would be pretty cool. Could I get a cardboard cut-out of Antoine too, do you think???

ME: Guys, come on . . . 😳

AMBER: 🤣 OK, OK . . . I think we're done. Soooo, erm . . . what??

ME: I accidentally invited him! I didn't mean to, I just meant it in a general kind of way, but he got the wrong end of the stick.

JESS: Have you told your parents?!

ME: NO!!

MOLLY: Well, I think you might have to . . .

ME: I can't, I'll be grounded for life or quite possibly killed 💀

POPPY: Yeh, and you don't want to end up on the Naughty List this close to Christmas! You'll never get your Airwrap then . . .

JESS: Ooh and what about Daniel?! What do you think he'll think if he finds out Antoine is coming to stay with you for Christmas??

ME: Jess, stop making this worse!!

JESS: SOZ xx

(8.25 p.m.)

How to deal with the Antoine situ:

1. Pretend I am back in hospital with more pus-filled boils.

2. Tell him we've moved house.

3. Tell him we've moved country.

4. Actually move house/country.

5. Put head in sand and pretend it's not happening.

I'm going with option 5 because it's easier/cheaper than moving house/country and, despite what he says, I'm sure he must be joking, because no one just turns up with their entire family to spend two nights with virtual strangers – do they?! That would be MAD.

PS It's far too late to go to the beach to find a patch of sand to bury my head in (and I'd be slightly worried about how I would breathe in any case) so I'm just putting it under the covers of my bed, which is much warmer and less messy. I also have my phone too or else I'd get bored.

WEDNESDAY 14 DECEMBER

Jess came round after school today and we found a mega box of Ferrero Rochers in the kitchen. Assuming Mum left them out for us as a snack, we took them up to my room and proceeded to eat ~~some~~, ~~quite a few~~, ~~most of them~~, OK, OK, all of them.

It wasn't too bad though – we shared them so it was only twelve each. It was actually quite educational as we had a fierce debate as to how you eat them.

I eat them in the only way that they should be eaten, which is a seven-stage process and goes like this:

1. Bite off all the outside chocolate until only the wafer shell is left.

2. Remove one half of the wafer shell.

3. Eat it.

4. Lick/eat chocolate filling until you discover the hazelnut.

5. Eat the hazelnut.

6. Lick remaining chocolate out of remaining shell.

7. Eat remaining shell.

Jess's process is . . . and I can barely even write this . . . a
ONE-STAGE PROCESS:

1. Put entire thing in mouth and chew.

Absolutely shocking scenes

That's it!!! It should be illegal. Maybe it is illegal in some countries. I mean, **WHO DOES THAT??!!?**

After we'd finished them (soz, Mum) I asked her what she would do about the Antoine situation.

'Well, I would have made it clear he wasn't invited in the first place.'

'Helpful!'

'Well, it's true. Why didn't you just tell him no?!'

'I did!! I explicitly told him he couldn't come but he said they'd already booked flights.'

'WHAT?! I mean . . . maybe he's joking?'

'You think so?'

She looked thoughtful. 'Yeh. There is no way his parents would just book flights without checking with your parents first, right?'

'I guess . . .' I said, smiling to myself.

THOUGHT OF THE DAY:
I feel a lot better about everything now.
I'm sure Jess is right, and Antoine is just
playing a trick on me, thinking he's funny.
Well, HA HA, Antoine, the joke is on you,
because I've got your number, buddy, and
I'm not falling for anything!

THURSDAY 15 DECEMBER

Whoop! Tomorrow is our last day of school, and everyone is feeling super pumped for the Christmas holidays. Even the teachers seem really excited (probably for different reasons) and we did almost no work all day. In English we did a Christmas-themed quiz, in drama we watched *Scrooge* and in art we made tie-dye style wrapping paper. It felt a bit like being back in primary school again, in a good way.

My last lesson was double science, which was as boring as ever because if there is one teacher who never makes lessons fun it's Mr Murphy. Weirdly it ended up being my favourite part of the day though, because about twenty minutes before home time, just as I was about to nod off, I felt a tap on my shoulder. It was Tia, who sits on the table next to me. 'This is for you,' she said, passing me a note.

'Thanks,' I replied. I held it underneath the desk so that no one could see, and unfolded the paper. A big smile crept across my face as I filled out my answer and added a cute little drawing of a reindeer.

Then I passed it back to Tia, hoping that it would make it all the way to the back of the class without being intercepted.

After a couple of minutes had passed, I decided to take a peek backwards and check on the note's progress – I instantly met Daniel's eyes. He had the note in his hand and a massive grin on his face.

I grinned back and, in that moment, the whole world seemed to stop. It was just me and Daniel grinning at each other in double science. No one else seemed to exist.

'Daniel Evans and Lottie Brooks,' said Mr Murphy, rudely interrupting our magical interlude. 'Something tells me that you are not listening to my highly riveting lesson on atomic structure . . .'

'Sorry, I am, sir,' said Daniel quickly.

'Me too, sir,' I agreed.

'Then why are you staring at each other with stupid grins on your faces?'

The rest of the class started whistling and laughing and I cringed deep inside.

'I guess we are just really excited about Christmas, sir,' explained Daniel.

Mr Murphy rolled his eyes. 'Well, I would hope you can curtail that excitement for another fifteen minutes or so while I finish telling you about the roles of different subatomic particles. Now . . .'

BLAH BLAH BLAH.

I obviously had zero interest in the roles of subatomic particles so I spent the rest of the lesson daydreaming about maybe, possibly getting back together with Daniel Evans.

FRIDAY 16 DECEMBER

EEK! Today is the day we get our Secret Santa gifts and we are also allowed to wear Christmas jumpers to school instead of our stuffy blazers. What do you think of my new jumper?? **I LOVE IT!!**

What is it about avocados that is so goddam cute?! I mean, essentially they are just a knobbly green not-very-attractive-looking piece of fruit. But when you add eyes and cut them in half so that their stones look like podgy bellies, then they are instantly ADORBS.

Walked into tutor group this morning and Mr Peters was dressed as Father Christmas!! I cringed a bit, but I couldn't help but smile too. It was pretty sweet that even though we were all thirteen years old (or nearly thirteen) he still tried to make it fun for us.

'HO HO HO, good morning, everyone! I hope you've all been very good this year,' he said. 'Please drop your gifts in this sack on your way in and I'll start giving them out once everyone has arrived!'

He looked and sounded so ridiculous; we all found it hilarious.

I put my gift into the large hessian sack he was holding and said, 'Morning, Father Christmas! Thanks for coming to visit us at such a busy time of year.'

That made everyone laugh even harder, but Mr Peters didn't seem to mind. In fact, it looked like he was really enjoying playing the clown for once – I mean, let's face it, it has to be pretty dull teaching maths all day, right?!

I'm not going to lie, we were all buzzing and looking forward to finding out what gift we had got. I grinned to myself, thinking about how happy Jess would be when she opened hers.

When everyone had finally arrived, Mr Peters picked up the sack, hauled it over his shoulder and started handing out the gifts one at a time. It was really fun watching what everyone got. Some people just got sweets and chocolate but they seemed pretty pleased anyway. When Jess got hers she opened it excitedly and said 'I love it!', then she announced to the class: 'Thanks to whoever got me these!'

I covered my mouth with my hands and grinned. Maybe I'd tell her it was me later, maybe I wouldn't. Hmm.

Everyone else seemed really happy with their gifts. Molly got a lip balm and nail varnish and Poppy got some Christmas tree socks and a pack of candy canes.

When Amber got hers, she said 'OOH, for me!' and made a big song and dance of opening it really carefully and excitedly. However, when she pulled out the present inside (a bottle of peach-scented perfume), her face fell, and she could not hide her disdain . . .

I don't think she meant to announce it to the class but she said it FAR too loudly and Mr Peters heard.

'Amber!' he exclaimed. 'That's quite ungrateful. Someone has put a lot of time and effort into getting that gift for you.'

'Sorry, sir,' she said, pouting, 'but I'd have to disagree . . . Everyone who knows me knows that I only wear designer perfume.'

'Everyone had the same gift limit of five pounds, Amber,' Mr Peters said, clearly losing his patience. 'Now if you need any further clarity on the matter then perhaps you should come and discuss it with me after school . . .'

She smiled sweetly and said, 'That's fine, thanks, sir,' and then under her breath, 'I suppose I can regift it.'

Mr Peters sighed and put his hand back into the sack. Reading the label on the last present, he said, 'And last but not least we have the ever-patient Lottie Brooks.'

I grinned and took the present gladly, quickly tearing off the wrapping paper. Then I just stopped and stared.

I could hear titters of laughter all around me and people nudging each other, saying stuff like . . .

'OMG, did you see what Lottie got?!'

'Brilliant – it's a novelty turkey hat!'

'Ha, ha! It's SO Lottie!'

I hate everyone looking at me and laughing so I started to go red, but I was also kind of upset. Whoever had bought me this Secret Santa clearly wanted to make me look silly.

Mr Peters must have noticed my face and the class's reaction. 'Is everything OK, Lottie?' he said, looking at the gift in my hand.

'Yes, everything's fine, sir,' I said, putting on a smile.

'OK, if you are sure?'

'Honestly, sir,' I said, and then I fake-laughed. 'It's funny.'

It wasn't really, but there was no point making a fuss, so I just stuffed the hat in my bag, put a brave face on and made my way to geography.

In the afternoon, instead of our usual lessons we had a special Christmassy assembly. It was all fairly standard stuff – Mrs McCluskey did a speech about the meaning of Christmas, what a wonderful year we'd all had at Kingswood High and how proud she was of us all – blah blah blah – and then we sang a bunch of carols. Just when I thought she was about to wrap it all up and dismiss us, she said, 'And for a final Christmassy treat, a few of our wonderful staff members have prepared something extra special. So, without further ado, please give a warm welcome to the Jolly Hollies.'

'The Jolly Hollies?!' I whispered to Jess.

She looked confused and shrugged at me.

Then the curtain came up. There was Mr Peters standing centre-stage, still dressed in his Santa suit, Mr Bishop sat behind a set of drums, dressed as Rudolph, Mrs Dodson on the keyboard was dressed as a snowman (or snowlady in reality – bit sexist calling them all snowmen when you think about it, right?) and this is the weirdest bit – Mr Murphy on the guitar was dressed as the Grinch!!

I was so shocked at this strange sight that I did not know how to react, so I just stared at them completely dumbfounded.

And then – AND THEN – Mr Peters started singing 'All I Want for Christmas is You' a cappella, all Mariah-style, before the rest of the band joined in.

It was one of the craziest, funniest sights of my entire life. They sounded awful but brilliant at the same time and the whole school was going crazy for them. By the end of the performance, we were all completely out of breath from jumping around, cheering and laughing so much.

'HAPPPPYYYYYY CHRRISTMAAAAAAAS, MR PETERS!' I shouted as they all waved to the crowd and disappeared off stage.

'Well, that was –' said Molly, not knowing how to explain what she'd just seen.

'Yeh, it was totally –' agreed Poppy.

'It was fantastically . . . CRINGE,' stated Amber.

'Fantastically CRINGE is absolutely what it was,' said Jess.

I laughed. 'Right, come on, guys, school's out for two weeks so we gotta celebrate – any ideas??'

'FRYDAYS!' they all chimed at once.

After we'd collected our orders, we walked home, eating chips and comparing our Secret Santa gifts.. Everyone was happy with the gifts they'd received – except me (and, obviously, Amber).

'Have you worked out who got you your lovely hat yet?' Molly asked me.

I pouted. 'No, I have no idea. But it must be someone who doesn't like me.'

'Oh, don't be so serious, Lottie. I think it's a thoughtful gift!' said Amber.

'She's right. It's SO you!' nodded Poppy.

'Urm . . . that is not a compliment!' I replied.

'Come on, put it on!' Jess grinned. 'You'll look brilliant. I think the person who bought it KNEW how hilarious you can be – in a good way.'

'I'm not hilarious on purpose, it's just accidental,' I argued, but I had to admit, they were talking me round.

I took the hat out of my bag and looked at it . . . Maybe the girls were right. Maybe it was quite a fun present after all.

Then they all started chanting . . . **'PUT IT ON! PUT IT ON!'**

'OK, fine. You win.' I put it on my head and fastened it under my chin and the girls immediately burst into fits of laughter.

Suddenly enjoying the attention, I bent my legs, tucked my arms up like wings and started walking in a jerky motion while clucking and bobbing my head.

The more the girls laughed, the more exaggerated my movements became.

I was so consumed by my incredible impression that I didn't notice that I had started to attract a larger audience . . . OR my friends trying to warn me of the extra attention.

I was a turkey. I was **LOVING LIFE**, and no one was going to take that away from me!

'Lottie? Lottie! LOTTIE! MAYBE YOU SHOULD STOP NOW,' said Jess, moving her fingers across her neck in a mock beheading.

'What's the matter?' I said. I was quite annoyed. I was enjoying myself, so why was she trying to ruin my fun??

'Ummmm, you might want to look behind you,' said Poppy.

I paused, still crouched down, my wings mid flap – suddenly very aware of how stupid I must look . . .

I knew I couldn't stay like this though. For one thing, my entire body was bent at unnatural angles and it was starting to hurt. I stood up slowly and turned round to see Daniel and Theo on the opposite side of the road laughing – AT ME.

'Don't stop on our account!' shouted Theo.

'Lottie, that was brilliant!' said Daniel, clutching his stomach.

I snatched the hat off my head. Brilliant. Just brilliant. Of all the people to see that – it had to be the guy I maybe have a crush on, didn't it?

THOUGHT OF THE DAY:
Whoever got me that stupid present has a lot to answer for!!! The only positive is that we've got no school for two weeks now so at least I can hide from everyone in my Fort of Shame. (I'll make sure I bring a box of Ferrero Rochers with me though, tee hee.)

SATURDAY 17 DECEMBER

9.25 a.m.

I was having a nice lie-in on my first day of the holidays
when I was jolted awake by people screaming at silly o'clock
in the morning. It turned out to be my brother and sister
taking it in turns to shout 'BAAA!' and 'BUM!' (or TBF not
even taking it in turns), so I went downstairs to politely ask
them to keep the noise down.

Luckily Mum then informed me that they are about to leave to go early-morning Christmas shopping, so if I didn't want to join them (I did not) then maybe I could go back to bed and enjoy the peace and quiet instead (I would like that very much).

(10.23 a.m.)

I had just about got back to sleep when the phone started ringing. ARGH, I thought, this is just what I need after a VERY stressful/traumatic week!

I considered leaving it to ring, but then I remembered that it could be an emergency or one of my friends with some exciting gossip. So, I ran down the stairs and managed to get to the phone before it stopped ringing (which I now massively regret). This is how it went:

Me: Hello?

Lady on phone: *Bonjour! Comment allez-vous?*

Me: Um . . . I think you might have the wrong number.

Lady on phone: *Non, je ne pense pas. C'est Lottie?*

Me: What?!

Lady on phone: *C'est Lottie?*

Me: I'm called Lottie, yes. But who are you?

Lady on the phone: *Je suis la mère d'Antoine. Nous sommes rencontrées en vacances en France.*

Me: *La mère d'Antoine?!*

Lady on phone who is actually Antoine's mum: *Oui! Bonjour, Lottie!*

Me: OH NO OH NO OH NO!

Antoine's mum: *Je ne comprends pas.*

Me: Um um um um um.

Antoine's mum: *Puis-je parler à ta mère? Je veux parler à ta mère de la visite pour Noël.*

LONG PAUSE.

Me: Sorry – what??

Antoine's mum: Errm, how say . . . may to speak your mother lady. I like to say thank you please for your invitations for our *famille* to do visitations in Englishman country.

OMG OMG OMGGGGGGGGGGGGGGGGG!

Me: *NON!* *Non.* My mother lady is out shopping.

Antoine's mum: *Oh, em . . . I téléphone cet après-midi?*

Me: *NON!!!* No, you can't call this afternoon because she is always out shopping. She's obsessed with buying stuff . . . shoes, mostly . . . she's rarely ever here actually. I can't remember the last time I even saw her . . . it was probably in a shoe shop . . . two months ago.

Antoine's mum: Ahhh, if *problème* to speak to mother lady, I must ask you . . . Is OK for *ma famille pour vous rendre visite pour* Christ Mouse?

Me: NO! *NON!* NON VISIT FOR CHRIST MOUSE.

Antoine's mum: Ha ha! *J'aime* the funny
Englishman humoursity.

Me: I wasn't jok–

Antoine's mum: *Au revoir, Lottie. À bientôt!* Tell
mother lady I bring a nice fish.

Then she hung up and I ran into the garden, and I screamed
until I became a public nuisance!

TQOEG WhatsApp group:

ME: URGENT MESSAGE INCOMING!!

POPPY: Uh oh. What have you done now?

AMBER: Is this more Antoine/Daniel drama because no offence but YAWN 😴

ME: Bit rude, Amber!

AMBER: Everyone's thinking it . . .

ME: No, they aren't!

AMBER: Are you getting bored of the constant Antoine/Daniel drama?
- ○ Yes   1
- ○ Also yes   3

AMBER: See.

ME: Jess?!

JESS: There was no other option to vote for, soz!

ME: OK, well I'm sorry, everybody. I'll try and mix it up a bit conversationally in future but right now I need your help. Antoine's mum just called, and they are definitely coming for Christmas.

MOLLY: WHAT?!

ME: I tried to tell her no, I really did . . .

POPPY: And what did she say?

ME: She said she'd bring a fish!

MOLLY: WHAT?!

AMBER: 😑 This is the problem, Lottie. Have you ever asked yourself why you keep finding yourself in these ridiculously silly situations??

ME: Errr, it's not just me, you guys do silly things too . . .

AMBER: Really? Has anyone else ever invited an entire French family that they hardly even know to visit them for Christmas . . . with a fish?!

JESS: Errr, no.

MOLLY: Nope.

POPPY: Don't think so . . .

ME: Well, thanks for the advice, friends!

MOLLY: Look, Lotts, we all love you, but what I think Amber is trying to say is that you've got to come clean before you make things 10,000 times worse.

JESS: I hate to say it but I kinda agree.

ME: But I don't wanna! ☹

AMBER: Lottie – you need to woman up and face the music!

ME: OK, OK, but if you never hear from me again it was nice knowing you and I leave everything to my hamsters.

POPPY: OOH, but can I get your flying squirrel onesie??

MOLLY: Yellow Air Force 1s for me pls?

JESS: Dibs the unicorn slippers and Justin Bieber cereal bowl!

AMBER: Don't worry about me. Not sure you have much I'd actually wear . . .

ME: Wow, cheers, girls. ☹
I'd best get writing my will then.

10.33 a.m.

The family are home, and I am hiding in my room like a scaredy-pants bunny rabbit.

I can hear them downstairs talking and putting croissants in the oven. I want a croissant, but I also don't want to be murdered, so unsure what to do?

Amber is right. I have to woman up. I have to tell the Fun Police. I am going to go downstairs and do it. I just need to blurt it out and deal with the consequences. Putting my head in the sand is not going to cut it. I must be brave! Wish me luck.

10.54 a.m.

I'm going now . . .

10.55 a.m.

I'm about to put my pen down . . .

10.56 a.m.

I've put my pen down.

10.57 a.m.

No, I haven't because I can't put my pen down if I'm still writing with it, can I?! Doh.

11.00 a.m.

OMG! I'M SO SCARED!!! BYE!

I couldn't do it. I tried. I really did try but Mum wasn't in
a very good mood as she was having to wash all the food
shopping as it was covered in sick. Apparently, Bella vomited
at the tills in Tesco and the pile of puke kept moving down
the conveyor belt, and then when it got to the end it all got
jammed up and broke. They ended up making an urgent
clean-up announcement on the Tannoy and they had to
move all the disgruntled customers to other lines.

Toby was super excited about the whole thing. 'You should
have seen it, Lottie – it was SICK, literally.'

Mum not so much. 'It was only marginally less embarrassing
than when she made Santa bleed.'

Anyway, yeh . . . not a good time.

SUNDAY 18 DECEMBER

LA LA LA. Put my head back in the sand!

Everything is fine, everything is fine, everything is fine.
If you keep repeating it, then that makes everything fine
(apparently).

'How is everything going, Lottie?' I hear you ask.

'EVERYTHING IS FINE!' I reply – because it's true.

Today is the day of Toby's Nativity at church. By the way
everyone is acting you would think Toby had the lead role in
a West End musical.

If I have to listen to him say 'BAAA' one more time, then I
will scream. It's already put me right off sheep, an animal I
was rather fond of in the past. Now whenever I see a sheep,
I just feel annoyed. **THANKS FOR RUINING SHEEP FOR
ME, TOBY!**

The good thing, though, is he looked totes ridic in his
costume. Obvs Mum thinks it's adorable, but it does

absolutely nothing for his street cred (which is already poor at best).

4.22 p.m.

Well, that was . . . interesting?!

We arrived at the church and Mrs Tomlinson (Toby's teacher) was in a total tiz-woz, as my mum would say.

Someone had forgotten to bring baby Jesus with them and 'you can't have a Nativity without baby Jesus!' – apparently.

Mrs Tomlinson was desperately running up and down the pews trying to see if any of the little kids had brought a doll with them, but sadly no one had. Then she came over to us with a strange glint in her eye.

'I don't suppose we could borrow your baby?'

'What? You mean . . . Bella?!' said Mum, looking shocked.

'Yes, she'd not have much to do, she'd just have to sit quietly in a crib for five or ten minutes,' explained Mrs Tomlinson.

'Well, she's not exactly –'

'PLEASE, you'd really be helping us out.'

'OK, I don't see why not . . .'

'You are a life-saver!' said Mrs Tomlinson, before disappearing to get the children ready.

I turned to Mum. 'You don't see why not?!'

'It'll be fine, Lottie.'

'Erm, have you seen Mary? She's eight years old and she is meant to give birth to a nearly one-year-old angry mutant baby who is loud and violent and TBH not very much AT ALL like baby Jesus?!'

'I mean, I guess you have a point, but what was I meant to do? They were desperate.'

I shrugged. 'I don't know . . . but don't say I didn't warn you when it all goes wrong!'

'I'm sure it'll be OK – stop catastrophizing. Anyway, I'll be back in a minute. I've got to take Bella backstage and get her costumed up – how exciting! Soon we'll have three actors in the family!'

'Good luck, Bella!' I said, giving my sister's squishy arm a gentle squeeze.

She looked at me, grinned and said, 'Bum!'

Oh, **GAWD!**

I turned to Dad, and we gave each other knowing looks, but I guess Mum was right about one thing – it was done now and we'd just have to cross our fingers and hope for the best.

Right – let's skip to the action!

Mum returns to our pew, Bella and Toby are safely deposited backstage. The Nativity begins!

It's all very nice TBH, just your standard kinda thing: poor old Mary and Joseph taking that long ride on a donkey, no room at the inn, arriving at the stable, kids looking cute with tea towels on their heads, an assortment of barn animals . . .

The narrator says, 'During the night, Mary gave birth to Jesus. She wrapped him in strips of cloth and laid him in a manger full of hay.'

Luckily, we didn't have to witness the actual birth. Instead Mrs Tomlinson comes on stage holding Bella and places her in the manger.

The audience collectively says, 'Ahhhhhhhhhhh . . .' – the fools!

Me, Mum and Dad watched on nervously.

'Now just lie still for two minutes, Bella . . . that's a good girl,' muttered Mum under her breath. I realized she was gripping my arm pretty tightly.

As we were in church, I said a quick prayer to God to the same effect and Dad had both sets of fingers crossed. The narrator continued: 'Nearby on a hillside, some shepherds were watching their sheep. They saw a bright light and an angel appeared.'

A cute little angel walks on to the stage, dressed in white coat-hanger wings and gold tinsel wrapped around her head as a halo. 'Do not be afraid. I have some great news – the son of God has been born in a stable in Bethlehem,' she says.

It's Toby's big moment. He walks down the aisle with a couple of tea-towel-headed kids and arrives on stage.

'Baaaaaaaa,' says Toby the sheep. He delivers it clearly and relatively realistically – he grins at us, pleased with himself, and we all give him a thumbs up.

The shepherds gather round the manger and look at

Jesus (Bella). One of them says, 'The prophecy is true! We are humbled to look upon our Saviour!'

Bella sits up in the manger. At first she seems quite confused, then she raises her face towards heaven as if she truly is the son of God and then shouts (very loudly) the word . . .

The vicar claps his hand over his mouth. Mrs Tomlinson looks horrified. The grandparents in the audience gasp. The children erupt into hysterics.

'Oh gosh, oh no,' says Mum.

Dad lets out a deep breath and looks hard at his shoes, avoiding all eye contact.

Mum turns to the congregation. 'Don't laugh at her,' she pleads, 'it will only encourage her.'

And it does. Spurred on by the reaction, Bella grins . . . 'BUM! BUM! BUM!' she shouts, clapping her little hands together.

The acoustics of the church make it sound ten times louder.

'BUUUUUUUUUUUUUUUUUUM!' Bella screams, absolutely thrilled with herself.

Mrs Tomlinson, trying to remain calm, says, 'It's time for our first hymn, "Away in a Manger".'

The orchestra begins playing and we start to sing. I guess they were hoping that Bella would be drowned out by the noise, but it only makes her more determined.

'BUM! BUM! BUMMY BUUMMMMMY BUM!'

Mum rushes up to the altar, picks Bella out of the manger and announces, 'Sorry, everyone. She's never said that before. She's only eleven months old. I've no idea where that even came from.'

I mean, Toby taught her it obvs, but if she's in denial then that's fine.

Mum runs back down the aisle and out of the church, clutching Bella, who is still shouting '*BUM*' at the top of her lungs.

Both the vicar and Mrs Tomlinson look totally bewildered. I'm not surprised, TBH – this is a Nativity, Jesus has been forcibly removed from the building for screaming obscenities and the kings haven't even visited him yet.

'I'm so sorry about that outburst, everybody,' says Mrs T when the hymn is over. 'We will continue with the performance shortly but, before we do, can I check if anyone has anything we could use as a substitute baby Jesus?'

Everyone looks around at each other and shrugs. Then a mum in one of the back pews stands up. 'I mean . . . if you are desperate . . . my daughter Harriet has this? I'm sure she won't mind you borrowing it.'

She holds up a large plastic pterodactyl and Harriet pouts. (I think she did mind.)

The vicar claps his hand over his mouth for the second time.

Mrs T looks pretty horrified too, but what else can she do but take it?!

Are they really going to continue the Nativity . . . with a pterodactyl?! I thought.

They were and they did. After rather awkwardly trying to stuff it into the crib – not easy, given its large wingspan – Mrs T ended up having to stamp on it, which made Mary Magdalene and little Harriet cry.

Thank goodness for the distraction of a child dressed as a big gold star, appearing and guiding the three kings to the stable! Once they were there, they bowed down to the plastic pterodactyl – sorry, I mean Jesus – and bestowed on him gifts of gold, frankincense and myrrh.

I think there was meant to be another hymn after that, but Mrs T was clearly keen to wrap everything up, so it all came to a rather quick end, the children took a bow and that was that.

Me, Dad and Toby met Mum outside the church doors. She was clearly shaken.

'How did the rest of it go?' she asked. 'Did anyone notice what Bella said?'

'Did anyone notice?! Of course they noticed she shouted the word BUM about 127 times!' said Dad.

'Right, well . . . it was a really lovely performance apart from that. Well done, Toby. You were great,' said Mum.

'Yeh, well done, bro,' I said, patting him on the back. 'That is the most realistic baaing I've ever heard in a nativity.'

'Really?'

'Uh huh.' I grinned. 'It was unbaaaalievable!'

'I agree,' said Dad. 'It must have been all the research you did on Ewe Tube.'

'They are right.' Mum laughed. 'I know there were a couple of bits that didn't go to plan, but remember – all's wool that ends wool.'

It was funny but, man, we are all SO cringey.

Then we got in the car and Toby sang 'A Bum in a Manger' all the way home with backing acoustics from Bella. It was only a five-minute journey but the singing made it feel like five hours.

MONDAY 19 DECEMBER

Met up with the girls in town to do some Christmas shopping, but we got kind of bored and spent most of the time sitting in a cafe, drinking gingerbread hot chocolates – mmmm.

We were all discussing our holiday plans when I heard my phone ping and saw Daniel's name pop up. I shot out of my seat and shouted . . .

'Calm down, Lottie. You're not on *Love Island*,' said Amber.

'Sorry, I just got a bit overexcited,' I explained.

'Really? We couldn't tell,' said Amber sarcastically.

'Sooooo, what does it say??' asked Molly.

They looked over my shoulder and I let them read the message.

> **DANIEL:** Hey, bit busy with family stuff this week, but wanna hang out next week? Maybe cinema or ice-skating? x

Amber slumped back into her seat. She really didn't like me having everyone's attention.

'Say yes, say yes!!' said Poppy.

I wrote a quick reply telling him I'd like that, and I could see him typing back immediately. I felt a nervous shiver pass through my body.

'He's replied already,' shrieked Jess.

'You lot really need to get a life,' sighed Amber, scrolling through TikTok on her phone.

PING!

> **DANIEL:** Cool! I'll drop you a message next week. Also, Theo is having a NYE party at his house if you are free? Poppy, Molly, Jess and Amber are welcome too x

Molly read it out loud to the group and that finally perked Amber up.

'A New Year's Eve party!' she said, grinning. 'I'm in!'

Everyone else was really excited about it too. I'd never been to a NYE party before (not counting family ones btw) and I just knew it was going to be so much fun!

TUESDAY 20 DECEMBER

Granny and Grandad phoned, and they have definitely decided to come and stay because they can't face the prospect of eating a nut roast on Christmas Day. Granny says she really enjoys coming to us for Christmas anyway, as our house is always nice and cosy and relaxed.

Mum said, 'It's only cosy and relaxed because she gets to sit on the sofa under a blanket and get cups of tea brought to her!'

As Auntie Emily and Auntie Claire were meant to be hosting Granny and Grandad, Granny invited them here too, which Mum said was a bit presumptuous. It also means that Mum will have to cook a nut roast AND a turkey (and possibly Antoine's mum's French fish).

'I'm actually glad,' I said. 'I thought it was going to be pretty boring with just the four of us.'

'Five!' said Mum. 'Have you forgotten your baby sister?'

'No, I'm just trying to block her out after Sunday's . . . events.'

'Fair point, but it's her first Christmas so we need to make it super special for her.'

'Mum, she's not even one. She won't remember anything . . .'

'It's the best age – next year she may not allow me to dress her up in novelty outfits.'

So, our Christmas of five has now turned into a Christmas of nine, and Mum is having to double her Christmas food shop. I was a bit worried about where they would all be sleeping. Mum said that Granny and Grandad would have their room and they would sleep on the sofa bed, then Auntie Emily and Auntie Claire would sleep in Toby's room, and he would sleep in with Bella.

PHEW! At least I still have my room to myself.

PS I know what you are thinking – maybe telling Mum that the nine guests may actually be thirteen might have been a good idea at this point . . . Have you forgotten my new approach already?

WEDNESDAY 21 DECEMBER

11.22 a.m.

Toby is worried that Gavin Sparkle-Balls is dead!

I went to investigate and realized that he hadn't moved for an entire week now. When I asked Mum why he wasn't doing any of his 'hilarious antics' any more, she snapped at me: 'Because Mummy's got enough on her plate without having to worry about that (insert swear word) elf.'

BLIMEY! So, he's now an '(insert swear word)' elf, is he? Poor old Gav – I actually felt quite sorry for him so I have brought him to my room for some R&R and sat him next to the hammies for company.

4.45 p.m.

I screamed!

I had put Gav S-B a bit too close to the hammies' cage and they have dragged his arm through the bars and amputated it at the shoulder. It must have been excruciatingly painful.

Toby and Mum came running to see what all the fuss was about. Toby was devastated when he saw what had happened. 'I thought you were looking after him,' he sobbed.

'Oh, Lottie! What have you done?' said Mum, looking cross.

'It was an accident! Anyway, it wasn't me, it was them,' I said, pointing at the Professor and Fuzzball the 3rd (who incidentally didn't look AT ALL bothered).

'Can we fix him, Mum?' asked Toby.

'I think Lottie should try and fix him,' said Mum, raising her eyebrows at me.

'No problem,' I said. Even though it was quite a big problem, as it wasn't like I could get the hammies to regurgitate his arm, was it?!'

(6.35 p.m.)

I've glued Gav's stump shut with some UHU glue and that's the best that I could do. I've also told the hamsters that there is absolutely no point hoping for a new see-saw this year because trying to eat one of Santa's official helpers will definitely mean they are on the Naughty List.

THURSDAY 22 DECEMBER

I was woken up way too early by Jess on the phone.

'Lottie, guess what . . . **IT'S SNOWING!'** she shouted down my ear hole.

'So?!'

'So . . . do you wanna build a snowman? Or . . . a snowlady?'

Reader, I did not want to build a snowman or a snowlady. I was snug as a bug in a rug. What I wanted was to be back asleep.

This did not please Jess. 'There is plenty of time to sleep when you are dead – how often does it snow here?! Come on, look outside – it's amazing!'

She had a point, I guess, so I reluctantly crawled out from under my duvet and peeked through the curtains. Overnight our garden had been transformed into a winter wonderland. It was a beautiful sight – except for the fact that my mother and brother were having an argument right in the middle of it. I opened the window so I could hear what they were going on about . . .

Mum: Toby, I'm not going to tell you again. You cannot make snow models of private parts!

Toby: Why not??

Mum: Because it's . . . rude! What will the neighbours think if they see?

Toby: They'll think it's hilarious!

'What's with all the shouting?' asked Jess, still on the end of the phone.

'Oh, just the usual. Mum's not happy because Toby has made a giant snow sculpture of . . . well, let's just say something quite inappropriate in the middle of the lawn.'

Jess laughed. 'Well, let me in and I'll help you both make something more family-friendly!'

'What do you mean "let me in"?'

'I'm standing outside your house with my spade. Did you not get the memo, Lottie?! I'm **VERRRRRRY** excited about the snow.'

I groaned and ran downstairs to open the front door.
After my initial reluctance, we had a really fun afternoon making a snowlady who we named Stephanie. It was harder work than I thought because we didn't have a huge amount of

snow to start with and it was melting quickly – I think we
did a decent job though. She had beach pebbles for buttons,
a traditional carrot for a nose and a pink neon wig that Mum
had bought for an 80s fancy-dress party.

By the time we had finished, my hands were almost frozen
solid, so Mum called us inside and said she'd make hot
chocolates to help warm us up. As we sat down at the
kitchen table to drink them, we realized Toby was missing.

'He was here a minute ago,' I said to Jess.

Then we heard a tap on the kitchen window. I peered
through the glass to see Toby proudly standing by Stephanie
and her new . . . additions.

'OMG, he's given her boobs!' shrieked Jess.

I sighed. 'Will he always be this immature?' I asked Mum.

At that moment Dad came into the kitchen, looked out the window and burst out laughing. 'Nice one, Tobes!' he said.

Mum rolled her eyes. 'Probably, Lottie. Probably.'

FRIDAY 23 DECEMBER

(3.34 p.m.)

Granny, Grandad, Auntie Emily and Auntie Claire have all
arrived. They immediately went to put their feet up in the
lounge because they were very tired from a long car journey,
and Mum went to make some tea.

When she brought it in – with a Tesco's Victoria sponge
(which looked amazing!), Granny said, 'Oh, shame it's not
home-made, but never mind.'

Mum muttered, 'It is the FINEST range.'

'Hmmm, they always taste a bit synthetic to me.'

'Is it vegan?' asked Auntie Emily.

'No, why?' said Mum.

'Me and Claire are vegan now . . . oh, and Claire is also
gluten-free. That won't be a problem, will it?'

'No. No problem at all,' replied Mum through gritted teeth.

'I accidentally ate a gluten-based mince pie the other day and I was on the toilet for two days straight,' explained Auntie Claire.

'The smell,' said Auntie Emily, 'it was like something out of –'

'Right, well, we best avoid that then,' interrupted Mum. 'So what can I get you that's vegan and gluten-free?'

'How about gin?' Auntie Claire suggested.

'Unless it's too early?' asked Auntie Emily.

'It's never too early for a G&T – especially at Christmas!' said Grandad.

Dad offered to go and make gins, and that seemed to wake everyone up a bit (except Grandad, who promptly fell asleep).

BLIMMIN' 'ECK. You'll never guess what has happened. Mum has well and truly had to say goodbye to her 'nice quiet Christmas' because this evening, just before 6 p.m., the doorbell rang.

I went and answered it, because Dad was busy making yet another round of G&Ts and Mum was busy trying to make an emergency vegan curry for dinner.

'Hello?' I said when I saw a man, lady and a small child standing there.

He looked and sounded vaguely familiar – suddenly the realization dawned on me. 'Uncle Tim . . . Auntie Sally?'

'Yes! And this is your cousin Frankie.'

I looked down at the little girl with blonde pigtails. She was super cute.

'My name iz Fwankie and I'm fweee years old,' she said, grinning up at me.

'Hi, Frankie! I'm Lottie and I'm thirteen.'

'You iz a big gurl!'

'Ha. Yes, I am.'

Dad appeared behind me then, looking white as a ghost.

'Tim . . . is that really you?' he stuttered.

'Brother! Long time, no see. I'd say the years have been kind, but you have even less hair than the last time I saw you.'

They both laughed and fell into a big bear hug.

It turns out that Uncle Tim, Auntie Sally and my cousin Frankie had flown all the way from New Zealand as a surprise. It was the first time we'd seen them in four whole years and the first time we'd ever met Frankie. It was a pretty emotional reunion and even Mum seemed thrilled . . . initially . . . until they revealed they hadn't booked anywhere to stay.

You could see the horror behind her eyes as she tried to work out where everyone was going to sleep and how the Christmas dinner was now going to have to feed twelve people (or sixteen if you count Antoine's family, the Rouxs, but, shhhhhhh – head in sand, remember) . . . though she hid it well. Kinda.

So off went Dad to buy another bottle of gin and everyone had a brilliant time catching up and swapping stories. Personally, I'm really pleased as it feels lovely and Christmassy to have such a full house!

8.23 p.m.

Dad has taken all the rellies to the pub, largely because the extra bottle of gin didn't last that long, and Mum's vegan curry burnt to a crisp during the reunion (I expect everyone was relieved, as it smelt awful).

I stayed behind to help Mum sort out all the sleeping arrangements and look after the kids, and that's when she broke the bad news. Not only would I have to give up my room, but I'd also have to bunk in with my siblings AND I'd have to share a double airbed with Toby!

I said, 'Sorry – WHAT?!'

'There is no other way round it, Lottie. We are full to bursting here and I've nowhere else to put you.'

'Come on, sis, it'll be fun,' said Toby. 'We can stay up late and have a farting contest.'

'BUM!' said Bella, as if agreeing.

'YAY!' said Frankie. 'I like doin' windy botty pops!'

God help me.

9.45 p.m.

What with the farting and howling, it's like going to sleep in a barn! They are SO loud and every time they quieten down little Frankie comes running in to offer her 'contribution' –

she may look adorable but the stench is horrendous. I mean,
what are they feeding that child?!

PS Toby keeps saying he is going to 'pull an all-nighter' and
I'm scared he's actually serious.

(10.13 p.m.)

They are still going! I tried leaving the room and sleeping in the
hall, but the adults aren't being much better either. The walls
of the house are vibrating, they have the music up so loud.

I crept downstairs and asked them to lower the volume, but
Uncle Tim and Dad grabbed me by the hands and started

twirling me round to some hideous old-people music by a band called Blur.

11.07 p.m.

Have made a bed in the bath; it's cold and hard but at least no one is farting in here.

It's all fun and games until someone has to sleep in the bath.

SATURDAY 24 DECEMBER

7.59 a.m.

Sleeping in a bath: one star. Do not recommend.

My back and neck are really hurting AND I kept being rudely woken up by people wanting to use my bedroom to do their teeth or go for a wee!

Still, you know me – I don't like to complain and ANYWAY who cares . . . because today is a v. v. exciting day – **HAPPY CHRISTMAS EVE, PEEPS!**

1 sleep to go – wahoo 😊

2.13 p.m.

The house is full. It's fuller than full. It's about to explode with people (hungover people, if you want to be specific).

Mum is constantly on edge; Dad is either making coffees,

teas or G&Ts, or hiding in the garden shed for increasingly long periods of time. Cousin Frankie keeps following me around like a little puppy, wanting me to play LOL dolls with her. I told her I couldn't play as I didn't have a doll and she pointed at Gavin Sparkle-Balls and said, 'You be 'im!'

I'm not a total meanie, I've tried my very best, but her doll, Partee Gurl, keeps being violent to my 'doll', poor old Gavin, and if Gavin retaliates at all, or even expresses an opinion that maybe Partee Gurl should stop hitting him (perfectly reasonable IMO), then Frankie gets really cross!

I don't think it's a very nice game for a three-year-old to play but I guess that's up to her parents to decide and they'd gone to the pub (again).

Oh well, at least I'll get a little bit of a break from her later because we are going to see *Aladdin* at the panto and she doesn't have a ticket – ha!

6.22 p.m.

There was no break. Frankie started crying when she found out she couldn't come to the pantomime so Dad said she could have his ticket – thanks, Dad!

I didn't exactly enjoy the show because I had to sit next to Frankie, who kept jabbing Partee Gurl into my leg and laughing.

Mum loved it because the genie was played by Scott, a guy from some 1990s boyband who she used to have a crush on. She was singing along to all the songs really loudly. I hope no one from school saw.

Afterwards, she made us wait in line for an hour so she could get her programme signed by him and then she told him that she used to be in love with him, and then she asked for a photo and gave him a kiss on the cheek – I was mortified. Especially when she nearly fainted. I don't think I've ever seen her so excited.

YUCK.

In the car I reconsidered telling Mum about the potential French invasion in less than twenty-four hours, but she was so busy WhatsApping her mum-friends the selfies of her and Scott that she wasn't really listening.

I'm sure it's all some sort of elaborate prank anyway, right? No one would think it was OK to just show up at the house of a family they barely know on Christmas Day . . . would they?!

LA LA LA. Head in sand. Everything's fine.

6.37 p.m.

OMG! Frankie went quiet for twenty minutes and it turns out she was cutting Gavin's legs off with a pair of scissors.

When I complained to the 'adults', Frankie insisted, 'No, it wurnt Fwankie what dund it. It was Partee Gurl.' For some reason they all found this totally hilarious.

'Oh, right, well, that's OK then, is it?' I said. 'Gavin's only got one limb left now – what's Father Christmas going to think when he sees this, Frankie? He's not going to be very happy with you, is he?'

Then Frankie burst into tears, and I got into trouble for being mean to her. Never mind poor old Gavin and what he's just been through. No one cares about him!

To cheer everyone up after 'the incident', Dad put on
The Snowman, which everybody seemed to enjoy apart from
Partee Gurl, who thought it was 'poopy'.

Afterwards, I helped put out the Father Christmas treats
with Toby, Bella and Frankie. We have a special plate that
we use every year decorated with holly, reindeer and
Christmas trees. On it we placed milk, cookies, a couple of
Quality Streets and some reindeer food, which I helped Mum
mix up – our secret recipe is porridge oats and glitter.

After the littlies had all gone to bed for the night, Mum said
I could stay up for a bit longer and watch TV with the adults.
She even let me try a sip of her Prosecco but it was so
disgusting I spat it right out.

I said, 'That is **SO** gross. I'm never going to drink alcohol –
EVER.'

She laughed and said, 'Well, we'll see if you change your
mind when you are older.'

I definitely won't!!

Oh, man. I thought they were all already asleep, but I just found Toby and Frankie in the downstairs toilet. He was feeding her spoonfuls of the magic reindeer food.

'I thought it might make her fly,' he told me when I asked what he was doing.

'Iz yummy!' said Frankie. 'I like a be a flying Fwankie!'

I just left them to it. Fingers crossed that the glitter isn't toxic.

Uncle Tim caught Frankie (just in time) before she tried to jump off the top stair.

Auntie Sally had to explain that the reindeer food wouldn't make little girls fly and that she might break a bone if she tried that again, then she took her back to bed. Maybe they should Sellotape her to the mattress or something.

(10.07 p.m.)

Goodnight!! Got to get myself to sleep before the Big Guy pays us a visit – keep all your fingers and toes crossed for a Dyson Airwrap for me, please! x

SUNDAY 25 DECEMBER

I know it's your birthday, Jesus, but please help me!

Toby has woken up approximately every thirty minutes all night asking, 'Is it Christmas yet?'

I keep telling him to look at the clock but he says he can't tell the time yet, even though the clock is digital – I really fear for that boy in later life.

To the best of my knowledge Bella has not slept at all. Every time I look at her she is standing at the bars of her cot staring back at me and chanting 'bum' repeatedly. At least she's whispering but it's really quite freaky.

I really wish she would learn another word TBH – any word would do, I'm not fussy!

I had finally got back to sleep when I heard the creak of the
door and I opened my eyes to see a silhouette of Frankie
holding Gavin and a large kitchen knife.

'OH MY GOD! WHAT ARE YOU DOING?!' I shouted,
rushing over to grab the knife out of her hand.

She grinned back at me. 'I cuttez hims uvva arm off – HA
HA!'

Now he just a bodee
and an 'ead!

I was horrified. 'Frankie – that's SO dangerous. Hasn't anyone ever told you not to play with knives?!'

'Fwankie like a play wiv a knives!' she said proudly.

I returned her to Auntie Sally and Uncle Tim's room, explaining what had happened, but they barely even opened their eyes. Then I returned the knife to the kitchen and put poor old Gav's limbless torso and head on the top shelf of the bookcase. He looks utterly defeated.

Luckily, I found some ear plugs and an eye mask in the bathroom cupboard, so I am going to put them on. The only way I am going to get any sleep is to try and block out everyone and everything.

I HOPE HOPE HOPE that this is the last time I will be disturbed. I cannot face another night in the bath; my neck is still killing me.

4.21 a.m.

OMG! Woke up and Bella was on top of me, staring into my face shouting 'BUM'! How did she get out of her cot??! I have no idea. She must have woken Toby up too because he

appeared at the other side of my face shouting, 'IS IT
CHRISTMAS YET?!'

I have told them it is not, and they must go back to sleep, but I
don't seem to have much authority over them.

4.38 a.m.

Gave up trying to sleep so I took my *roommates* downstairs.

I didn't mind too much about the early start as I was desperate
to see if I'd got the Airwrap. We aren't allowed to open presents
until our parents are up but I'd memorized the dimensions of

the box, so I came downstairs armed with a tape measure.

However, it all turned out to be pointless as when we opened the door to the lounge the sight that greeted us was NOT good. Frankie was standing by the tree, covered in chocolate and surrounded by wrapping paper.

She had opened ALL the Christmas presents and eaten ALL the Christmas-tree chocolates.

She grinned at me and said 'Fwankie likes a choc choc' as if that were a good explanation for everything.

I felt like crying. Toby did cry. Bella just shouted 'BUM' (obvs).

5.04 a.m.

I have sifted through the mound of presents and wrapping paper and although there is no Airwrap, there is a REALLY good-looking dupe version. I'm SOOOO happy and super excited. I cannot wait to use it later! I've hidden it under some other pressies so that Mum won't know I've seen it and I can pretend to be shocked when I get it.

'OTTTTIEEEE! OTTTTIIIIIEEEE! FWANKIE DOOOOD A BIG SPAWKLY POO! COME AND AV A LOOKY!'

I would like to say I declined but unfortunately my curiosity got the better of me and sure enough, in the toilet, Frankie had indeed produced a large glittery poo. I knew feeding her the reindeer food was a bad idea!

Toby pushed me aside. He had an aquarium net in his hand (RIP Rick and Morty 2016–2017, gone too soon, never forgotten).

'What on earth are you doing?!' I asked him as he plunged the net into the toilet bowl.

'Fishing it out,' he told me as if I was stupid.

Frankie squealed and started jumping up and down with excitement.

'I see that – but WHY?!'

'Well, you know the story of *The Goose that Laid the Golden Egg*.'

'Yeeeeeeeeeh.'

'Well, this is pretty much the same – *The Frankie that Laid the Golden Turd*! It might be worth a lot of money.'

'What?! Don't be so –'

I'm not going to lie, I couldn't even come up with a reply – it was still FAR too early to be dealing with that.

Kids are SO gross.

Took Bella into the lounge and put her in her Jumperoo while the others continued to play their bonkers version of hook-a-duck.

I must have dozed off or something because next thing I knew Bella was halfway up the Christmas tree. I reckon when she's older she could go on *Britain's Got Talent* as an escapologist or something.

'TIMBER!!!' shouted Toby from the doorway just as the whole thing came crashing down.

Bella was completely unharmed and unfazed by her mountaineering disaster and found the whole thing hilarious, but by now the lounge looked like it was the victim of a smash-and-grab.

6.49 a.m.

Even though we are technically not meant to wake Mum and Dad up until 7 a.m. at the earliest, I decided this was an urgent matter.

'All the kids are up and we've got a bit of an emergency,' I told them.

Mum picked up her phone and groaned. 'It's not even six o'clock, Lottie – can't you deal with it yourself?'

Funny how she only trusts me to be a responsible adult when she doesn't want to get out of bed . . .

'No. No, I can't. They've already totally ruined Christmas and their behaviour is out of control,' I said.

'What?!'

'Frankie's unwrapped ALL the presents and amputated Gavin's leg with a kitchen knife, Bella's destroyed the Christmas tree and Toby fished a glittery turd out of the toilet and put it in a Quality Street tin.'

'OH MY GOD!'

'It's Jesus's birthday, Mother. Don't be blasphemous.'

She rolled her eyes at me and started putting her dressing gown on. Dad was snoring through the whole thing.

I took her downstairs to the lounge and I tried to warn her, I really did – but I don't think she was fully prepared for the sight that greeted her.

10.33 a.m.

Mum draped a couple of throws across the presents and put *The Grinch* on the TV for the kids to try and distract them.

Then she drank four cups of coffee back-to-back hunched

over the kitchen table while peeling parsnips. She looked like she was about to keel over so I decided to be a good daughter and help her prep the rest of the veg.

As it was just the two of us, I took a deep breath and tried to talk to her. 'Mum, I think Antoine could be –'

But she just kept muttering stuff like, 'No, don't worry about me, you all lie in, I'll do EVERYTHING like ALWAYS!' so I gave up in the end.

It was after 10 a.m. before any of the other adults emerged from their pits, despite Mum crashing pans together and stomping around the house as loudly as she could. When Uncle Tim and Auntie Sally finally got up, Mum showed them the damage in the lounge and explained what had happened.

They said, 'Surely Frankie didn't open ALL of the presents?'

Frankie stood right in front of the carnage and very proudly announced . . .

'Yes, I dood do it! I ruins everyfing!'

Then they just started laughing and saying stuff like, 'Oh

gosh, what a little pickle!' I could not believe it – you can get away with murder when you are a cute three-year-old with pigtails.

When everyone was finally up, Dad offered them toast and Auntie Sally said, 'Oooh, I don't suppose you have any bacon, do you? A bacon sarnie would go down a treat!'

Grandad said, 'If you have any eggs I wouldn't mind a couple, sunny side up . . . sausage and mushrooms too . . . if you have them.'

'Now you're talking,' said Uncle Tim. 'Full English for me please, Bill!'

'Well, if everyone's having a fry-up, I may as well join in,' said Granny.

'A full vegan brekkie for me and Emily,' said Claire, smiling. 'Gluten-free toast for me, naturally!'

'Coming right up,' said Dad, trying as hard as he could to sound cheerful. Then I was drafted in to help. Toby was too busy looking up the price of golden turds on eBay. (I expect it's a slightly niche market.)

11.44 a.m.

Present-opening was a bit random. Mostly as they were all already unwrapped and secondly because no one seemed to remember what they had bought for anyone anyway.

Granny said the best thing to do was to just go and pick anything you liked out of the pile and that we should take it in turns from youngest to oldest. Bella was napping so Frankie got first pick and she went straight for MY hair styling tool even though she barely has any hair. I was livid.

Mum mouthed 'I'm sorry, I'll get you another one' at me from across the room.

MEGA SAD FACE!

I ended up with a saucepan set and an electric foot warmer. **WORST CHRISTMAS DAY EVER!!**

12.01 p.m.

Toby just came up to me and goes, 'Lottie, I'm sorry that you didn't get your hair styler.'

I looked at him suspiciously. 'Why are you sorry? What are you up to?'

'Nothing. I swear.' Then he looked kind of sheepish and pulled a box of Ferrero Rochers from behind his back. 'I got you these to say Happy Christmas and thanks for being a great big sister.'

He looked totes emosh and I felt a pang in my heart. How sweet of him to get me my all-time faves – it was a twenty-four pack too!

'Ahhh, thanks, Tobes,' I told him, taking the box, lifting off the lid and offering him one.

'No, don't worry. You deserve to eat them all,' he said, smiling.

I grinned and lifted one of the chocolates out. The morning had been super manic and suddenly I realized how starving I was. MMMMMMM.

I unwrapped the gold wrapper slowly to find . . .

I mean I was fuming, obvs. And I would get him back later.
But I had to admit it was a pretty decent trick – the size and
shape of the sprout was just spot on!

(12.13 p.m.)

TQOEG WhatsApp group:

AMBER: Happy Christmas, everybody! What did
you all get? I got a HUGE bottle of Chanel No5,
an iPhone 14 Pro Max, £500 cash, and a whole
bunch of Dior make-up.

POPPY: Lululemon shorts and a North Face puffa.

MOLLY: Some Drunk Elephant stuff and Pandora charms.

JESS: LOADS of books and footie stuff, OOH and an adopted meerkat!

I tried to stay quiet, but it didn't really work.

JESS: Lottie, what did you get?

ME:

MOLLY: A saucepan?!?!?

ME: 3, actually – various sizes.

AMBER: What's that thing on your feet?!

ME: It's an electric foot warmer . . .

MOLLY: Oh yeh, duh. Obviously.

POPPY: You asked FC for saucepans and an electric foot warmer?!?

ME: No, I didn't . . . I just . . . oh don't worry. It's a long story.

MOLLY: Okaaaaaay. We'll try not to. Anyway, any news on Antoine? Did he turn up??

ME: Not yet . . .

AMBER: He still could though, I guess?! Maybe he's on his way!

JESS: No, I reckon he isn't. He's got to be pulling your leg. Turning up like that on Christmas Day would be madness.

POPPY: Just ask him, Lottie – what have you got to lose?

ME: Um . . . EVERYTHING!!

I figured they were right though. What was the point of
spending all day freaking out when I could just message him
and ask him outright. I went to hide in the toilet so I could
concentrate and compose a message that didn't look like I
was COMPLETELY FREAKING OUT. Which of course I was. So,
I decided to go with complete denial . . .

> **ME:** *Salut, Antoine. Joyeux Noël!* I hope you
> had a lovely day, whatever you are doing. ☺
> L x

> **ANTOINE:** Merry Christ Mouse, dustbin! What are
> you speaking of? I am on my way to the house
> of Lottie at this instant moment, you silly spoon.
> I am looking forward to giving you a terrible gift
> which I'm sure you will be scared of. See you
> soonest, my marriage material! A xx
>
> PS I am actually thirty minutes of foot movements
> away.

OMG!!!!!!!!!!!!!!! WHAT AM I GOING TO DO?!?!??!

12.40 p.m.

TQOEG WhatsApp group:

ME: Head-in-sand strategy did not work! I repeat, head-in-sand strategy DID NOT WORK!

POPPY: ?!?!??! We need details???

ME: He's going to be here in twenty minutes.

AMBER: Hate to say I told you so! ☺

MOLLY: Well, I was going to watch some Christmas telly, but I might just hang out here instead as this is way better entertainment.

JESS: I'm about to microwave some popcorn.

POPPY: Me too – keep us updated!

ME: Will do. x

12.55 p.m.

I must keep looking at the clock nervously as Uncle Tim says, 'What's wrong, Lottie? You look like you are expecting the police to turn up and arrest you for murder!'

'Well, it wouldn't be the first time,' I told him.

'What?!'

'Nothing!'

I almost wished he was right, and that I had murdered somebody or at least criminally damaged someone else's property, but the truth was that I was stressing that Antoine was about to turn up at any minute.

'Muuuuuuuuuuuum,' I said, poking my head round the kitchen door.

'I am knee-deep in goose fat so unless you are dying, I DO NOT WANT TO KNOW!'

'It's just that I need to tell –'

'Lottie – are you dying?'

'Well, technically yes, because we are all slowly dying, but –'

'I DO NOT HAVE TIME FOR THIS. GO BACK TO THE LOUNGE!'

'There's not even anywhere to sit.'

'Well, go and sit on the stairs then.'

I sighed. And went to sit on the stairs. Maybe my gravestone could be engraved with: 'At *least I tried!*'

1.02 p.m.

A knock on the door! EEEEEEEEEEEEEEEEEEEEEEEEE EEEEEEEEEEEEEK!

It was nice knowing you!! x

1.36 p.m.

So that actually went really well!

That might be a lie.

It's definitely a lie.

Am I in a movie or something or is this my actual life?
Because sometimes I really feel like my life is so mad it HAS
to be a movie. Or *The Truman Show* or something like that.

This is why . . .

I ran to the door before anyone else could get there (not that
anyone else was trying – they were far too busy drinking/
cooking/trying to sell sparkly turds on eBay) and flung it open.

It was Antoine. I was half pleased to see him (he looked
dreamy) and half horrified. He was obvs NOT joking about
coming here for Christmas lunch – Mum was going to utterly
freak! I looked behind him and saw he was on his own – well,
that was one good thing, I guess.

''Ello, *ma belle Lottie!*'

'Antoine – what are you doing here?!' I whispered, pulling the
door closed behind me.

He grinned at me and then retrieved a stack of large
A3-sized cue cards from behind his back.

So, I consider your positives and negatives...

ANTOINE'S NUMBER 1 GIRLFRIEND!

I did not know how I was meant to react. It was quite sweet (in a way) but a lot of it was actually quite insulting?! So I just stood there gawping at him. Then I heard some whooping behind me, and I realized that all my relatives had their faces pressed up to the living-room window and they were clapping and cheering.

'What's going on here?' Mum was behind me, looking very confused. 'Antoine – is that you?'

'*Oui*, 'appy Christ Mouse, Madame Brooks!'

'Happy Christmas, Antoine! But what are you –' began Mum, before being interrupted by the rest of the Roux family coming along the street, calling out and waving at us.

'Ahhh, here come *ma famille*!' said Antoine.

OH NO.

Mum went white. 'What's going on, Lottie?'

'Oh erm . . . well, erm. . . Antoine . . .' I began to explain.

'Lottie invites us to join you for the drinking of alcoholic eggs from a glass! *Merci* for your invitations,' said Antoine.

Mum looked at me – I looked back at Mum. I wasn't sure
what to do so I just laughed nervously. Luckily (or unluckily)
at that point Monsieur Roux, Madame Roux and Hugo arrived
on the doorstep, with a frightening amount of luggage.

Antoine's mum and dad introduced themselves as Helene
and Philippe, and Helene opened up her suitcase and
produced a large Tupperware which she gave to Mum.
'*Merci*,' said Mum, taking the Tupperware and lifting the
lid to reveal a large sad-looking grey fish, complete with
eyeballs. 'Oh, wow – you really... shouldn't have.'

'Come in, come in – stay for a drink,' said Dad.

'Thanking you. We are staying for a night also. Very kind,'
said Philippe.

Mum by this point was almost grey – I was kind of worried she might drop dead from shock.

'You have a very 'orrible-looking house,' said Hugo, shaking my dad's hand, 'and it smell so 'orrible as well.'

'Oh, er – *merci*,' replied Dad, scratching his beard.

Then they came inside with their suitcases, and I didn't dare look my parents in the eye. Mum is always super polite – she won't kill me in public. I am scared for what she will do when we are alone again though . . .

1.56 p.m.

JESS: Lottie – what's happening????????????

POPPY: Come on – you can't leave us hanging like this?!

AMBER: I must admit, even I am vaguely interested . . .

MOLLY: Yeh, Lottie, where are you??!

ME: I'm hiding in the shed with my dad. Neither of us wants any drama, we just want to be left alone to live our lives in peace (we might just stay in here permanently).

POPPY: What about school though?

ME: There is no need for school if you are living in a shed for the rest of your life. The employment opportunities are pretty limited.

AMBER: You are being ridiculous again, Lottie. Just tell us what happened!!

ME: OK . . . so they are here. All of them. I feel a bit relieved that at least the worst bit is over.

MOLLY: But what did everyone say??

ME: Um, not really sure as I've been mostly hiding in the shed. I think the majority of people are kind of like, 'the more the merrier', except Mum as she's the only one doing any work.

POPPY: That doesn't sound too bad.

ME: Yeh well, Antoine also asked me to be his girlfriend again. Or more specifically, told me that I was his girlfriend!

JESS: You can't just instruct someone that they are your girlfriend! I hope you told him where to go!

ME: Err, well, I just went and hid in the shed. Anyway, I'd better go. Dad said he doesn't think we'll get any Christmas dinner if we stay in here and we've already finished all the sausage rolls he's smuggled in.

MOLLY: One more thing – did they bring the fish?!

ME: Yes – it was a horrible, miserable-looking thing and it still has its eyes!!

JESS: Ewwwwww!

2.18 p.m.

I apologized 127 times to Mum while helping her in the kitchen. I promised to clear up after dinner and wash up too. I grovelled as best as I could. I don't think she has fully forgiven me, but she seems to have embraced the situation (a bit) and is much more chilled out than she was this morning. I suspect it's partially down to the number of glasses of Prosecco she's had since breakfast.

The main problem we are faced with now is that there is no way near enough turkey or chairs for everyone. Last week we were expecting there to be five people for dinner and now we have sixteen! Mum said we'd be lucky to get one slice of turkey and two potatoes each, so we put the fish with eyeballs on a baking tray and shoved that in the oven too.

2.45 p.m.

The Roux family seem to be getting on incredibly well with everybody. I mean, I don't want to blow my own trumpet but maybe, actually, this is turning out to be the most fun Christmas we've ever had?!

Hugo is pretending to be a lion and giving all the little ones rides on his back and Antoine is currently teaching all the adults how to breakdance. Even Grandad is joining in, and he never voluntarily gets out of his armchair!

3.24 p.m.

Just found Frankie and Bella in the laundry cupboard surrounded by empty chocolate-coin nets. Frankie was feeding them to Bella – with the foil still on.

'How many has she had, Frankie?' I asked.

'Three,' she replied.

'Oh, good. That's not too bad.'

'Three billionty million,' she said with a grin.

'POO!' squealed Bella.

'Oooh, I didn't know you could say that!'

'I teach 'er 'ow to say poo!' said Frankie. 'Do I get a tweat for it?'

'No. No, I don't think you do,' I told her.

So, dinner was an interesting experience . . .

Dad brings out the turkey and everyone starts clapping him and saying 'Bravo Bill!' and 'What a cracker!' – Mum's jaw practically hit the floor.

I stood up and said, 'I think we should all give Mum a clap too, considering she cooked it all!' I think Jess would have been proud of me. Also, I was still desperately trying to win some good-daughter Brownie points.

Dad was about to carve the turkey and then Granny said we should get a group photo while the table looked so lovely, so we all huddled together behind the turkey and Uncle Tim set up his camera with a timer.

Dad said, 'Everybody say "Happy Christ Mouse!"' and as we did that, Bella projectile-vomited all over the turkey. It splattered over the whole thing. You should have seen everyone's faces. Or, well, you can . . . because there's a rather epic photo . . .

Mum said she could probably wipe most of it off, but no one found the thought of eating turkey very appealing after that so it basically just went in the bin. Auntie Emily and Auntie Claire were super smug with their nut roast but everyone else had to make do with one pig-in-blanket each, one roast potato, a spoonful of fish and a whole lot of parsnips and sprouts.

Being the kind daughter I am, I volunteered to forgo my share for a chicken-and-mushroom Pot Noodle. Antoine and Hugo seemed happy with the deal too. Toby opted for twelve chicken nuggets and Frankie got an entire selection box with a few carrot batons for nutrients (which she put up her nostrils).

When the adults had finally sat down at the table, ready to eat (please note that all the kids were actually standing or sitting at the breakfast bar as there weren't enough chairs), Philippe stood up and raised his glass. 'I like a make a cheers!' he said. 'I ask Hugo to make Englishman words for me.'

Everyone clapped as Hugo stood up too and waited while Philippe explained to him what exactly he wanted to say. A few minutes later, Hugo cleared his throat and began to speak.

'My family say, thank you for welcoming us into your small, overcrowded home where there is not enough furniture. You people are not ones we would ever choose to be social with in a normal world but we felt forced to accept your Christ Mouse invite, so here we are with no chance of escape! Life is a funny old sausage – ha ha . . .'

My mouth was hanging wide open at this point!

'So we thank God, Jesus, Beard Man and *la famille* Brooks for giving us these tiny, oh so tiny, amounts of foods which look and smell like a dying animal on a hot day. And even though we didn't want to come . . .'

WHAT THE?!?!?

'We didn't want you to come either!' I shouted out crossly.

Everyone burst out laughing at my 'joke' even though it wasn't meant to be funny.

Hugo ignored me and continued . . .

'Well, that's the strangest speech I've ever heard,' said Dad, laughing and raising his glass. I don't think anyone else really noticed or cared that Hugo and Philippe had actually insulted everyone and everything, because they all raised their glasses too and shouted, **'CHEERS, IDIOT GEEZERS!'**.

Then we all ate and TBH it was the nicest Christmas dinner I've ever had. Can't beat a Pot Noodle – apart from the fact that Mum nearly ruined it by putting a sprout in each pot, probably to make it seem a bit more festive. I threw mine down the toilet when she wasn't looking.

5.45 p.m.

After dinner there was a moment of calm. I thought about returning to the shed but it was getting a bit boring in there, so I wandered through to the hallway and found Antoine sitting on the stairs.

I sat down next to him. We hadn't spoken properly since he got here. Too busy, no time . . . the fact that I'd been hiding in the shed a lot. I guess if I'm honest, I'd been avoiding him.

'Hello, number-one girlfriend,' he said, putting an arm round me.

'Hey, Antoine, how's things? Have you had a good day?' I replied.

'*Oui, ma petite* dustbin.'

Then we fell silent for a minute or two before he said, *'J'aime le fromage.'*

I smiled. 'I like cheese too, Antoine, but I think we already know that about each other, right?'

Did we really have nothing else to say to each other?! I looked at him. No one could say he wasn't good-looking or charming or kind.

I was hit with the sudden realization that there was, in fact, more to life than cheese (I think?!) and that I needed to break it to Antoine that I didn't want to be his girlfriend. It was a horrible thing to do on Christmas Day but there was no way round it.

I called Hugo over and asked him for help translating what I wanted to say.

'Hugo, please can you thank Antoine for his very kind offer of me being his number-one girlfriend, however I'm going to have to say no. I'm not sure a long-distance relationship is going to work, especially with the language barrier. I hope that we can still be friends.'

'Oh yes, of course I tell him,' said Hugo.

Hugo speaks in French to Antoine for a minute or so and then Antoine gets up and storms down the stairs and locks himself in the toilet.

'What did he say?'

'He is very full of regret. He wishes he had chosen Amelie instead.'

'Oh.'

Antoine is fine now. I put my turkey hat on and did a silly impression for him and all is forgiven. He said I will always be his little dustbin no matter what, so that's nice.

Shortly after he'd agreed to come out of the bathroom (where I strongly suspect he was on the phone to Amelie) there was another knock at the door and Toby shouted, 'There's another one of those boys holding cards here for you, Lottie.'

'WHAT?!'

This is where it all gets really strange . . .

I went to investigate, and it was Daniel – holding cue cards just like Antoine.

'Hi, Lottie,' he said. 'I really like that hat on you, you know.'

URGH. I had forgotten about the turkey hat again! However, it was too late to take it off now, and it was pretty warm and comfy, so I kept it on.

I smiled and said, 'Thanks, Daniel,' and then I started to read the cards as he held them up one by one . . .

Dear Lottie,
   Because it's
Christmas, I just
wanted to say...

Then Daniel's face dropped, and I felt an arm on my shoulder
. . . Antoine had appeared in the doorway behind me.

''Ello,' he said to Daniel.

'Oh, um, sorry, I'd better introduce you –' I stuttered
nervously – 'Daniel, this is Antoine. Antoine, this is Daniel.'

The realization dawned on Daniel . . .

OMG!!!!! I pushed Antoine back inside.

'No . . . Daniel . . . I didn't . . . the language, it's a bit confusing
. . . I would never call you a . . . Brown Toilet Deposit. Antoine

and his family are here . . . as . . . family friends.'

Daniel tried to smile but I could tell he was embarrassed, and hurt. 'You don't have to explain. I shouldn't have just turned up unannounced. I just didn't realize that you and he were still –'

'We aren't, honestly there's nothing going on, he just –'

He didn't let me finish. He turned, let the cards fall to the ground and started to walk back down the garden path. 'Happy Christmas, Lottie.'

'Happy Christmas, Daniel,' I said to his back, even though I could tell he was too far away to hear me. 'It was good to see you.'

And then he was gone.

'Lottie! Pudding's ready!' I heard Mum shout from inside.

I feel so bad. It's all such awful timing . . . bit strange though, to be standing there with a turkey hat on my head and have two boys both wanting to date me!!

Pudding was laid out in the middle of the dining table for everyone to help themselves.

Dad clapped his hands together. 'We've got trifle, Christmas pudding, cheese and biscuits and a chocolate log!'

Everyone *oohed* and *ahhed* and started digging in.

'I didn't make a chocolate log,' said Mum, looking confused.

'That's strange, Toby said that's what was inside the Quality Street tin,' explained Dad.

Oh. My. Life.

It had Frankie's glittery poo in it!

I felt my stomach drop as I saw Hugo pick up the tin and start to take off the lid.

I looked at Toby, who was standing there wide-eyed and frozen to the spot.

Then I looked at Frankie, giggling in the corner. 'Iz my choc choc log! I did maked it wiv my bot bot!'

'POOOOOOO!' shouted Bella.

'Oh, lovely! She's learnt a new word!' said Mum.

I mean, your eleven-month-old daughter being able to say 'Bum' and 'Poo' is hardly something to celebrate, is it?! Still, I didn't have time to get into a debate about it. Hugo was staring at the contents of the tin in disgust. He had his spoon poised as if he was about to take a scoop.

I practically flew across the room and grabbed the tin from his hands.

'Actually, maybe don't eat that. I think it's past its sell-by date,' I shrieked.

'Don't be so dramatic, Lottie. I'm sure it's absolutely fine. I've just got it out of the fridge,' said Dad.

'EWWWWWW. TOBY?!?!'

Toby shrugged. 'I wanted to make sure it was kept nice and fresh.'

'It's not fine. It's OFF!' I said as I emptied it into the bin.

'Hey!' screeched Toby. 'I was up to £2.25 for that on eBay!'

If there was a competition for Most Disgusting Little Brother in the World, I swear Toby would win it hands down.

7.45 p.m.

To lighten the mood after the very average Christmas dinner, Dad got the Advocaat out and started making eggnogs for everybody. The Rouxs seem very excited to try it but they all agreed it was 'très dégoûtant', which is not a good thing. It didn't seem to affect their drinking of it, though, because by my counting all the adults are on their third one, which may help to explain why they are all dancing round (and on top of/ lying under) the dining table singing strange French songs:

I asked Hugo what they were singing about, and he said it's a popular children's song about plucking feathers off a nice bird. ☹

Why would you teach kids such a horrible song?!

Frankie has tied a piece of string around Partee Gurl's hand
and attached the other end to the top of Gavin's elf hat. She
is dragging them around together – and I'm not going to lie,
it's a pretty scary sight.

'What are you doing, Frankie?' I asked her.

'Gavin iz Partee Gurl's pet now!' she replied.

'Okaaaaay . . . and where is Partee Gurl taking Gavin?'

'She's takin' 'im to a vet to get 'im sum injections!'

I didn't think Gavin's life could get much worse, but
apparently, I was wrong.

And breathe – the Rouxs have left the building!

They decided not to stay, given the only accommodation we could actually offer them was a tent in the garden or the kitchen floor/bathroom. Luckily Dad managed to find them a room in a local B&B and we were all visibly relieved.

I think they had a nice Christ Mouse Day experience, but I doubt they'll come again, which is probably for the best. The most important thing was that everything turned out fine with Antoine and we promised to stay friends. Oh and get this – Hugo told me that he was on the phone to Amelie in the toilet and she agreed to go out with him, so I was replaced in a record-breaking forty-five seconds!!

As we were saying goodbye, Antoine ran back into the lounge and retrieved a beautifully wrapped gift from under the collapsed tree. It said 'To Dustbin, love of Antoine x' on the tag.

'Ahh, you shouldn't have,' I said, reaching out to take it.

He quickly pulled it back. 'Yes,' he said, ripping the name tag off. 'If you no mind, I give it to Amelie now . . . I give it to Amelie even if you do mind – ha ha!'

'Charming! I'm glad to know I didn't break your heart though.'

'No, you know Antoine don't do the feels of the heart!'

We both laughed at that and had a little hug.

After that, the whole family waved our French friends off and
closed the door. Mum looked shattered so I bagged her a good
spot on the sofa and covered her in the electric blanket, gave her
a big glass of Baileys and told her to put her feet up for a bit
while watching telly. She was asleep in about twenty-five seconds.

Then we all decided to clean the house.

Auntie Emily mopped the floor, Auntie Claire did the hoovering, Auntie Sally loaded the dishwasher, Uncle Tim put the bins out, and even Granny did a light tidy-up of the lounge. Grandad said his knees were hurting and me, Toby and Dad were in charge of washing up (deffo the worst deal).

When Mum woke up from her nap, she was utterly thrilled – you should have seen her happy little face. She said it was the best Christmas present ever, so hopefully I have now well and truly redeemed myself.

I must admit, it did give me a warm fuzzy feeling inside too, which made me think that maybe I should help around the house more often. I mean, being thirteen now I do have a lot of responsibilities and stresses but I could probably offer her twenty minutes every other Tuesday or something?

(10.30 p.m.)

Everyone is super tired! It's been a crazy day. Toby and Bella are already fast asleep and I'm in bed and can hardly keep my eyes open.

But then I remembered about the cards that Daniel dropped on the doorstep . . . I needed to find out what the rest of the message said. So I dashed back downstairs, past the lounge full of snoozing rellies and quietly opened the front door.

Luckily, they were still there. I picked them up; the writing had smudged a little in the cold and damp but I could still just about make it out.

OMG! He likes me – he likes me quite a lot!

BEST CHRISTMAS DAY EVER!!*

*Apart from the fact that I may have completely ruined everything, because now he thinks I'm going out with Antoine – but I'll worry about that tomorrow . . .

MONDAY 26 DECEMBER

TQOEG WhatsApp group:

ME: Morning! I'm bored so I wondered if anyone fancies going into town? I'm fed up of eating crisps and chocolate and fancy a proper dinner.

POPPY: McDonald's?

MOLLY: Could murder a McChicken Sandwich. 12 p.m.??

AMBER: YES!!

JESS: WHOOP! See y'all there xx

Met the girls in Maccy D's and filled them in on the rest of Christmas Day and the Antoine/Daniel situ.

'What, so they BOTH turned up on your doorstep holding cue cards?!' said Amber.

'Yes, pretty much.'

'And what did you say?'

'I had to let Antoine down gently. But then when Daniel came over, Antoine called him a brown toilet deposit to his face and I sort of just stood there.'

'Oh God. Poor Daniel,' said Jess.

'Um, yeh. It was all a bit awkward.'

'And where are Antoine and his family now?' asked Amber.

'In a B&B. They are doing some sightseeing today, and then they fly home tomorrow.'

Amber sighed. 'Well, I think you've been quite selfish.'

'How has Lottie been selfish?!' asked Jess.

'She could have introduced them to us before kicking them out – I mean, did she even consider that me and Hugo could have been perfect together?! I've always dreamt of dating an older French guy and now it'll probably never happen.' She pouted.

'Oh, don't be ridiculous, Amber,' said Molly, which shut her up because Molly hardly ever tells her off.

'So, what are you going to do now?' asked Poppy.

'I don't know . . . it's all a bit of a mess. I was kind of hoping you guys might be able to help me? That's if you aren't too bored of the drama . . .'

'Nah, you came to the right people,' said Jess with a big grin.

'But this is your last-chance saloon . . .' warned Amber.

'Yes, boss!' I laughed.

TUESDAY 27 DECEMBER

Granny and Grandad, Auntie Emily and Auntie Claire, and
Uncle Tim, Auntie Sally and Cousin Frankie left this morning.
They are all going back to Leeds for a few days before Tim,
Sally and Frankie leave to go visit Sally's family in Newcastle.
It was an emotional goodbye and the adults all promised not
to leave it so long next time.

It was Frankie who was the most distraught about leaving
though.

'What's wrong, Frankie?' I asked her.

'Iz Partee Gurl who is sad,' she sobbed. 'She dun wanna leave
'er pet elf.'

I couldn't help letting out a laugh.

I took her little hands in mine. 'Frankie, would you like to take
Gavin with you?'

'Weally??'

'Yes, of course. That's if you and Partee Gurl promise to take good care of him?'

'I PWOMISE, OTTIE! U iz a best cuzin EVA!! I wuv you!'

'I love you too, Frankie,' I replied, giving her a big squeeze. And I meant it because even though she's utterly bonkers and a little bit terrifying she's also very cute.

I was lying on the sofa, having a nice relaxing afternoon watching *National Lampoon's Christmas Vacation* (which FYI is a GREAT movie) when Mum comes in with her hands on her hips.

'I want a word with you, Charlotte Brooks!' she said in her super stern scary-mum voice.

'Why?' I said. 'What have I done?'

Mum sighed. 'What have you done?!'

'Errrr . . . yes?' I really didn't like the way this was going.

'Well, how about inviting four random people to come for Christmas and not telling anyone about it, for starters.'

I shrank into myself. 'They weren't random. We met them on holiday,' I said weakly.

'You can't just invite everyone you meet on holiday to come for Christmas dinner!'

'I suppose not, but I said I was sorry.'

'Hmm, well, you can show just how sorry you are by writing the family thank-you cards.' She plonked down a big box of cards and a long list of names and addresses in front of me.

I looked down at the list – there must have been about fifty people on it!

'But Mum, this is going to take FOREVER!'

She smiled at me, patted me on the head and said, 'Well, you'd best get started then!'

URGH.

(6.27 p.m.)

Three hours of gruelling labour later and I can't even feel my right hand any more!

I found Mum in the kitchen and plonked the finished stack down on the breakfast bar. 'Done!' I told her.

'Great!' she said. 'And did we learn anything in the process?'

'I learnt that it would have been much quicker and easier to send a group email.'

She rolled her eyes. 'Anything else?'

'Don't invite random people over for Christmas dinner,' I said, while rubbing my painful thumb, 'as it may result in permanent damage to young delicate finger bones.'

Mum laughed. 'That's my girl.'

Just had a MEGA interesting FaceTime chat with TQOEG about a top-secret operation that will take place **TOMORROW**. I bet you're intrigued but I'm not going to tell you so you'll just have to be patient – ha ha!! All I will say is that it's going to involve quite a lot of confidence on my part, so I REALLY hope I can pull it off!

WEDNESDAY 28 DECEMBER

I'm standing round the corner from Daniel's house in the freezing cold, wearing my turkey hat. I look like a total idiot and I'm probably the most nervous I've ever been.

'I can't do it!' I say to the girls.

'Yes, you can!!' they all say in unison.

'But what if his parents answer?'

'Then just ask to speak to Daniel. It's not rocket science, Lottie,' said Amber.

'But I look ridiculous!'

'So – what's new?!' Poppy laughed.

They were right. I knew they were right. Daniel did the same for me so I had to be brave.

I took a deep breath and walked down the road towards his house. When I reached it I looked back and saw the girls hiding (badly) round the corner. They all gave me the thumbs-up and mouthed, 'GO!'

I walked up the front steps and pushed the doorbell before I could change my mind.

The waiting was agony but before long I heard footsteps approaching. *Please be Daniel, please be Daniel,* I pleaded.

The front door opened. 'Lottie?'

'Daniel?'

It took a few seconds for me to recognize him as he was wearing a novelty Christmas tree hat . . .

The good news was that he was smiling; I breathed a sigh of relief – he wasn't mad at me.

'I'm sorry about the other day. We had surprise visitors, and sometimes things don't translate that well . . . but me and Antoine, we are just friends.'

'It's OK, you don't have to explain.'

'I know . . . but I want to . . . so I . . .' I brought a stack of cue cards out from behind my back.

You won't believe how badly I was cringing on the inside, doing this, but I tried not to let it show . . .

Not everybody
knows this,
but I'm really
quite shy.

And I know that my face is turning bright shades of red.

I'd done it! But I wasn't sticking around to wait for his reaction. That would have been too much to take in one day. So I ran down the road back to the girls, who all cheered and high-fived me. I felt so proud of myself, and now I just have to wait and see . . .

THURSDAY 29 DECEMBER

It's not like I expected an instant response. I know he probably needs some time, but as much as my brain tells me to be sensible about it, my heart is hurting that I've not heard anything from Daniel **ALL DAY**. And then I start worrying . . . is it too late? Has he changed his mind? Does he even believe me? And can I blame him? I mean, how would I feel if I turned up at his house on Christmas Day to find a girl who he'd had a holiday romance with at the front door? And what if *she* called me a brown toilet deposit?!

I'd be pretty livid, TBF.

Oh no, maybe we are actually over for good?!? ☹

THOUGHT OF THE DAY:
Changed my mind about the electric foot warmer. I think it's the best present ever. I've had it on for about ten hours today watching Christmas telly with Mum. We have a perfect system going where we both put one foot in for thirty minutes and then we swap positions, so that the other foot doesn't get jealous. OOH and we also have a box of Ferrero Rochers (real, not sprout) that Mum remembered she had secretly stashed in the cupboard under the stairs – winner!

Love you, Mum.

Love you too, Lotts.

Heaven ☺

FRIDAY 30 DECEMBER

(12.45 p.m.)

Met the girls in Starbucks to discuss celebrating our first NYE out together. And of course – outfits.

The one fly in the ointment was that I STILL hadn't heard back from Daniel.

'I think he's just waiting to speak to you in person,' said Molly.

'Yeh, that's why you need to make sure you look EXTRA HOT,' agreed Poppy.

'Well, it won't be too hard to look better than the last two times I've seen him, as at least I won't be wearing that stupid turkey hat.'

'Hey, don't be so ungrateful!' Amber pouted. 'I spent a lot of time hunting for that.'

'What?!' I said.

'OOOOPSY,' she said with a grimace.

'I should have known it was you, Amber! I just hoped that maybe by now you'd consider me a better friend than that.'

'Oh, come on, Lottie. It was a joke. Just cos you're in a bad mood about Daniel, don't take it out on me.'

I sighed. She was right. I was in a bad mood about Daniel and I was looking for someone else to blame (and I had grown a little bit fond of my hat too – it was super snug).

'Lottie, you need to chill. We'll have fun tomorrow – with or without Daniel, OK?' said Jess.

'Yep, you're right – it's going to be the BEST NYE EVER!' I agreed.

'Errr, you shouldn't say that, Lottie! It's tempting fate!' screeched Poppy.

I covered my mouth with my hands, instantly regretting making such a bold statement.

'Don't worry, it's fine if you say *touch wood* at the end of the sentence.'

'OK, it's going to be the best NYE ever – **TOUCH WOOD.**'

'Now touch some wood.'

I tapped the table.

'That's actually laminate.'

She was right. I scanned the room for some proper wood but couldn't see any.

'Urgh, everything is made out of plastic these days,' tutted Jess.

'How about that tree?' said Molly, pointing through the window to a tree at the other end of the street.

'That's like . . . AGES away.'

'Well, do you want our NYE to be the WORST night ever?'

I sighed. 'Noooooo.' I needed to touch that tree.

I put my frappa-whappa-thingaling down and ran out of the door and up the street as fast as I could. By the time I got to the tree I was sweating, even though it was only two degrees outside. I leant on the tree to briefly catch my breath, and then I touched its bark and turned round to run back.

That's when I saw Daniel and Theo standing outside WHSmith, staring at me with confused looks on their faces.

'What are you doing?' Theo laughed.

OH GAWD!!!! What was I going to say?

(Probably should have said 'just having a walk' but hindsight is a wonderful thing and, you know me, I do like to waffle.)

Now Daniel was laughing too. 'And could you?'

'Could I what?'

'Run to the tree and back in thirty seconds?!'

I put my hands on my hips. 'Well, I don't know now, do I? You guys interrupted me.'

'Our apologies.' Theo grinned. 'Perhaps you should try it again?'

I grinned back and started walking towards the cafe. 'Maybe I will.'

'Well?' said Jess when I returned and plonked myself back into my seat.

'Well . . . I touched it, but some other weird stuff happened so I'm not sure it was actually worth it.'

'What stuff?' asked Poppy.

I looked back through the window. Dammit. Daniel and Theo had sat down on a bench by the tree.

'I'll explain later. I have to do it again, but faster. Can someone time me?'

'I guess so,' said Molly, getting her iPhone out and opening up the stopwatch. 'Just say when?'

I got into my starting position and imagined I was going for gold in a 200-metre sprint. 'WHEN!'

And then I ran like the wind, like my life depended on it, like I was Usain Bolt (but ~~slightly~~ significantly slower). I touched the tree. I barely looked at the boys but I could hear them clapping and cheering me on. 'See you tomorrow at my party, yeh?' called Theo. I gave him a thumbs-up sign and then I ran back to Starbucks just as fast.

'29.13 seconds!' announced Molly as I took my seat.

I punched the air. **'YES!'**

Jess giggled. 'Now are you going to tell me what on earth that was all about?'

I picked up my drink and slurped the remaining frappa-whappa-thingaling out of it. 'Well . . .' I began.

NEW YEAR'S EVE

(6.13 p.m)

Had a what-to-wear panic so I messaged my next-door neighbour Liv and she lent me a really cute little black playsuit that I paired with my Air Force 1s and gold hoop earrings. 'If you are unsure, always go classic,' she told me. EVEN BETTER, she had a Dyson Airwrap, so she curled my hair for me too and I'm so pleased with how it looks!

'It's great for loose curls that look natural but aren't natural,' said Liv, 'and it goes with your make-up, which looks "barely there" even though it is there, and your outfit, which looks like you haven't tried too hard, even though you have – geddit?'

I nodded my head eagerly. TBH, I didn't care too much what she was talking about as long as she was making me look better than my own attempts – which admittedly weren't too hard to top.

(6.35 p.m)

Time for a quick pep talk from the hammies and then I am off!

I should be asleep but I can't sleep until I've told you what happened. EEEEEK.

The prophecy of the tree outside WHSmith came true – it was the **BEST NIGHT EVER!**

Me and the girls arrived at around 8 p.m. and there were already quite a lot of people there. Mostly boys from the football team but The Sporty and Clever Girls were there too and a few other faces I recognized from school.

I saw Daniel chatting to a group of his mates in the kitchen and I felt really shy but as soon as I walked through the door he moved towards me and called out, 'Hey, Lottie – want a drink?'

'Sure,' I said, smiling.

I felt really pleased as I think this was the first time I've not had my mouth full of food when I've bumped into him at a party.

I know what you're thinking – yeh, it was a bit of a strange compliment. But if I complimented his hair back, then it wouldn't seem genuine, so I had to think outside the box. Plus, his nose did look good as noses go . . . no crusty bogeys visible, etc.

'Coke OK?' he asked.

I nodded. 'Coke's good.'

He poured some from a big bottle into a red plastic cup like they have at American college parties in the movies.

'Cheers,' I said, taking a sip. I felt really grown up.

I was at a cool party on NYE and I was having a drink with a boy I like – WOW!

'So, is there a name for your tree-based running . . . sport?' asked Daniel.

'Oh sure, yeh, it's very popular in some countries, especially Outer Mongolia. It's called . . . Treelay. Like Relay but with trees.'

I thought that was a pretty good name considering I'd just made it up on the spot, but Daniel sniggered. 'I thought a key component of relay races is that it's a team sport?'

I kept my face deadpan. 'Yes, well, in this case the team is me and the tree! Hence, it's called Treelay.'

'You are strangely hilarious, Lottie Brooks.' He grinned.

I couldn't fake it any more. I let myself laugh . . . 'So people keep telling me.'

'Hey, guys!' Theo bounced up to us and put an arm round both me and Daniel. 'Are we dancing – or what?!'

I looked around and the place had really filled up. Jess, Molly, Poppy and Amber were already on the dance floor (or in the dining room, if you want to be specific) and they were waving me over.

'Sure, let's dance!' I said as we made our way over to the others.

The night passed so quickly. Why does time pass so quickly

when you are having fun and so slowly when you are in double science – how is that even fair?!?!? I'd danced nearly non-stop for hours, with brief pauses to get some air in the garden or another Coke in my red cup.

I was just in the middle of busting some of my best moves to 'Levitating' by Dua Lipa when Theo shouted, 'Hey guys, it's midnight in a few minutes! We've got to do a countdown!'

Everyone started scrabbling around trying to find their besties so that they could see in the new year with their favourite people. I was already with Jess and Molly and we quickly found Poppy, who was stroking a cat in the hallway, and Amber, who was trying unsuccessfully to integrate herself with a bunch of Year Nines.

'Come on, guys, we all have to be on the dance floor for the countdown!' I said, dragging them through the crowd.

'OK!' shouted Theo. 'Ten –'

Hang on a minute, where was Daniel?!

Everyone joined in with the countdown – 'Nine – eight – seven –'

He was here just a minute ago . . .

'Six – five –'

I felt the disappointment start to creep in.

'Four – three –'

It had been a great night but I really wanted to be with him when the clock chimed twelve.

'Two – one –'

'HAPPY NEW YEAR!!!!!!!!!!!' everyone screamed in unison, just as I heard a familiar voice shout from behind me, and a pair of familiar arms squeezed my shoulders and pulled me into a hug.

I spun round, my eyes met Daniel's and the next thing I knew we were kissing. I don't know if he kissed me or if I kissed him, it seemed almost automatic – like two magnets drawn to each other.

We both pulled back and grinned at each other.

'Can I ask you something?' he said.

'What?' I said. It was quite hard to hear him above the celebrations.

'Would you like to go out with me?'

'Would I like to eat a trout with you?'

'No – I said, would you like to go out with me?'

'I'm sorry, Daniel, I'm just not a big fan of trout . . . or fish in general, TBH . . .'

'I didn't say that, I said – would you like to go out with me, as in – would you be my girlfriend?'

'You want to go out with a trout and make it your girlfriend?!'

This was turning into a seriously weird convo.

Daniel shook his head in frustration and then walked over to the DJ booth and grabbed the mic.

I stood there open-mouthed while everyone around me started clapping and cheering. I couldn't believe he had announced it to the entire party!

The room fell silent again and I realized everyone was staring at me.

Oh . . . I'm meant to say something, I thought.

So I said, 'I guess that would be . . . OK.'

And then Daniel ran back over to me, picked me up and twirled me round.

Now I'm back home, filling you guys in, and I still feel like I'm spinning. To be honest, I'm not sure how I'll ever stop!

(**2.01 a.m.**)

Yes, I know it's **SO** late and I really should go to sleep but then I remembered I only had a couple of pages in my diary left and that I should probably finish it off so I can start a shiny new one tomorrow. It is New Year's Day after all.

Plus, I was just thinking back to the start – do you remember when I said I had a feeling that this Christmas was going to be particularly epic? Well, was I right or was I right?!

'You were SO RIGHT, Lottie!' I can almost hear you hollering from wherever you happen to be right now . . . snuggled in your bed, curled up on the sofa . . . maybe even hunched over your school desk during reading time. Errr . . . what am I on about?! I keep forgetting that this is a SUPER PRIVATE DIARY for no one else's eyes but mine – which is a shame because I happen to think I have a very eventful life . . .

Anyway, I'm running out of space so let me get on with Lottie's Worldly Wisdoms (we are on part five now – wow!):

Dear Lottie,

Well, that was a pretty mad one, eh?! I don't think I've ever had a crazier or more chaotic Christmas holiday in my life! There have been some highs – me and dreamy Daniel are finally a thing, YAY – and some lows – Bella Bum Church Gate, the turkey hat, the golden turd, the elf massacre, the many, many unexpected guests, sleeping in a bath, I guess I could go on . . . BUT it all worked out OK in the end (kinda).

As ever, we've learnt some v. important lessons along the way . . .

★ *It's always best to be honest and not put off owning up to stuff – even bad stuff. The longer you leave it, the worse it will get – trust me!*

★ *Don't be afraid of looking silly or being silly – being serious all the time is just dull.*

★ *Be proud to wear novelty festive hats.*

★ *If you are mysteriously gifted a box of Ferrero Rochers by a sibling, check they are not sprouts before getting excited.*

* Cheese, although very yummy, is not enough to build a relationship on.

* Electric footwarmers are seriously underrated.

* So are Pot Noodles as Christmas dinner substitutes – YUM.

* Christmas is a time for family, and even if everything goes wrong . . . it really doesn't matter as long as you are with the people you love.

* But do not let baby sisters/plastic pterodactyls anywhere near a manger.

* Or LOL dolls anywhere near your elves.

* Finally, trees should be respected; they are wise, honest and great good-luck omens – especially the one near WHSmith, who I really do owe a massive thank you to . . .

I think there is only one thing left to say and that
is . . .

**MERRY CHRISTMAS AND A HAPPY NEW
YEAR, EVERYBODY!**

See you next year.

Love Lottie
xxx

KATIE KIRBY is a writer and illustrator who lives by the sea in Hove with her husband, two sons and dog Sasha.

She has a degree in advertising and marketing, and after spending several years working in London media agencies, which basically involved hanging out in fancy restaurants and pretending to know what she was talking about, she had some children and decided to start a blog called 'Hurrah for Gin' about the gross injustice of it all.

Many people said her sense of humour was silly and immature, so she then started writing the Lottie Brooks series.

Katie likes gin, rabbits, overthinking things, the smell of launderettes and Monster Munch. She does not like losing at board games or writing about herself in the third person.

EVERYONE
IS READING ABOUT LOTTIE'S EMBARRASSING LIFE. TOTAL NIGHTMARE!

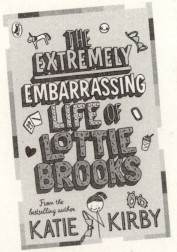
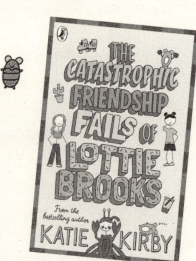

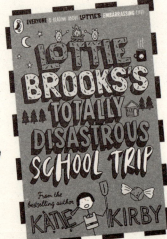

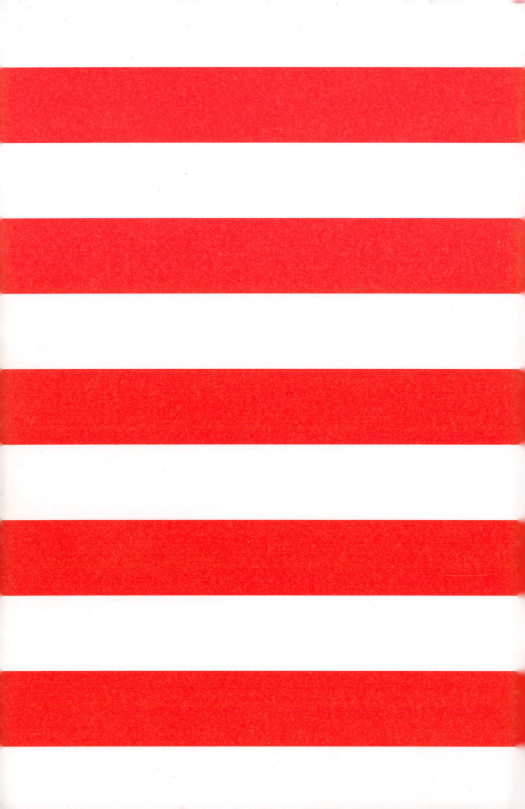